Second Chance on the Cove

A LATER IN LIFE ROMANCE

CHICKADEE COVE TRILOGY
BOOK TWO

ELIZA ESTER

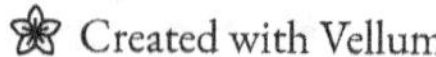 Created with Vellum

Chapter One

My wife?

The oven dinged. Dinner was ready. Jeannie glanced back at the kitchen and bit her lower lip. Suddenly, the hunger pangs she felt earlier dissipated. She was in no mood to sit down and eat.

The silence in the room was deafening. For a moment, Jeannie thought her ears weren't functioning right. They could practically hear a pin drop. Or perhaps it was her eyes. She couldn't tell. There was no way Luka was in her living room.

"I said, step away from my wife. Or did you not hear me the first time?"

Jeannie's eyebrows furrowed. She wasn't imagining it. Luka was actually in her living room. A million and one thoughts were racing through her mind. *Was this about Lily? Luka was with her the last time I saw him. What in the world would give Luka the audacity to step foot into my home?*

Aaron was still on one knee, confused. Jeannie herself was so confused, she froze. Her evening had gone from a romantic dinner to a scene out of a soap opera.

"Excuse me?" Aaron scoffed and rose to his feet. "Your wife?"

Luka crossed his hands. "I believe I was loud and clear. Get your hands off my wife. Now."

"Last I checked, Jeannie was divorced," Aaron said, still holding onto Jeannie's left hand. "You have no authority here."

"I think I have more authority than you here. We have children together, after all." Luka glanced at Aaron's hand again. "Get your hands off. I won't say it again."

His effrontery was flabbergasting. Jeannie could not utter a word. She refused to believe the same Luka who had walked out of her life with his head hanging in shame was the same Luka standing there with so much confidence. Almost as if he owned the house. As if he owned *her*.

Jeannie knew she ought to say something. She knew Aaron was waiting for her to say something. But she couldn't. Her mind hadn't fully processed what was happening. A part of her was waiting for Luka to laugh and state he was merely joking.

Finally, Aaron took his hand off Jeannie's. "I think you should leave. If you haven't read the room, we're sort of in the middle of something. It's rude of you to barge in here and make demands when you have no right to, don't you think?"

Luka chuckled and shook his head. "Look, man. I have no idea who you are to Jeannie. But I need to speak to my wife, and this show you have going on here doesn't concern me, either. Just step away from her. Maybe you can come back some other time." Luka turned to Jeannie with rheumy eyes. "Jeannie, we need to talk."

"About what?" Jeannie heard herself say. "Luka, what are you doing here?"

Luka gestured at Aaron. "We will talk when he leaves," he said.

"I'm not leaving," Aaron said, slightly irritated. "If anyone is leaving, then it should be you. From the look on Jeannie's face, she wasn't expecting you. You're the uninvited guest, and you should leave."

"Jenny?" Luka called her softly.

Don't call me that.

Jeannie would have said it if her lips weren't frozen shut.

Now they were both waiting for her to say something. Jeannie stared back and forth at the two men, feeling the heat rise in her throat. She didn't want to believe any of it was happening. Just a minute ago, she had her head in the clouds as she stared down at Aaron on one knee. They had just kissed. Her first breathtaking kiss in what seemed like forever. It was difficult to bring her head down from the clouds and back to reality.

Aaron reached for Jeannie's hand again and squeezed it. "Jeannie, what's wrong?" he asked quietly. "You're pale."

Before Jeannie could respond, Luka charged at Aaron. In three strides, he had his hands on Aaron's shirt and was shoving him away.

"I told you not to touch her, didn't I?" Luka rasped.

Jeannie gasped and was about to turn her attention to Aaron, who had staggered three steps back, when she saw the rage in Aaron's eyes. Jeannie recoiled, sensing that her living room was about to turn into a wrestling ring. Aaron reached for Luka and shoved him so hard, he fell to the floor.

"Aaron!" Jeannie blurted.

Jeannie's mind couldn't deal with violence. It frightened her and made her nauseous.

Luka scrambled to his feet, red with rage. "You little—"

"Stop!" Jeannie tried to yell, but her voice cracked. "Please, no fighting."

"Jeannie, tell whoever this is to leave," Luka rasped. "We need to talk. You and I."

Jeannie massaged her temple. "Is this about Lily?"

"Lily? No. Lily's fine. She's on a movie set till next week."

"Then leave," Jeannie said. "Luka, leave. Please. I am exhausted from all the yelling. You have no right to come here demanding anything. Honestly, I don't even understand where you got the audacity from. But right now, I don't want to know. Please leave."

Luka scoffed. "I'm not leaving."

"She asked you to leave," Aaron reiterated. "Don't you see that your presence is affecting her?"

"You might want to ask yourself why that is," Luka said and shrugged his shoulders. "We have history, if she didn't tell you."

"Yeah, traumatic history. I heard all about it. Leave, while she is asking nicely."

Luka turned to Jeannie. "Really, Jenny? You want me to leave?"

"I am this close to punching you if you don't," Aaron rasped, taking one step closer.

"I'm not leaving you here," Luka said and crossed his arms. "Like I said, I came here to talk to Jeannie. But seeing there's someone here trying to take advantage of her vulnerability, I'd rather stay. You know, just to make sure she's safe."

Aaron groaned and grabbed Luka by the shirt. He curled his fingers into a fist and was about to lift it when Jeannie screamed.

"Would you both, please...leave."

Simultaneously, they turned to stare at Jeannie. "Both of you. Leave my house," she repeated. "I'd like to be alone."

Aaron let go of Luka's shirt and walked toward her. "Jeannie—"

Jeannie stared at the ground trying to steady her

breathing. "Aaron, please leave," she asked in a whisper, stepping back.

Reluctant at first, Jeannie lifted her head. She could see the disappointment in his eyes before he stepped back and turned around. Aaron picked up his jacket and without saying a word, walked out of the house.

There was silence for a few seconds before Jeannie heard Luka gather his bags from the ground. He stood upright with them and waited till he locked eyes with Jeannie.

"I'll come by when you're calm," he said. "Good night, Jenny."

Even with the house empty, she still couldn't think straight. Perplexed, suddenly exhausted and confused, Jeannie trudged over to the couch and crashed on it. Her eyes were wide open—she had forgotten how to blink. Just a couple of minutes ago, she was dancing in Aaron's arms. Now, she was on the couch, drained.

And the oven was still dinging.

August, early '90s...

"How about Poppy? I think Poppy is a nice name for a girl."

"Luka, do you want our child to get bullied in school? Poppy? Who names their child Poppy?"

"Creative people do," Luka answered. "What? Poppy's a nice name. Very feminine. It's cute. Don't you think?"

"Yeah, when she's like five. Imagine an eighteen-year-old with the name 'Poppy.' Not so cute now, is it?"

Luka chuckled and wrapped his arms around Jeannie.

"Well, I thought it would sound nice with your name. Jenny and Poppy. Mother and daughter. Luka, Jenny, and Poppy."

Jeannie snuggled into his arms. "I like it when you call me Jenny. That's weird, isn't it?"

"It's not weird. I like calling you Jenny. Remember how that started?"

Jeannie smiled and shut her eyes. "Yeah, after we met in seventh grade, we were paired for a science project. I think that was when you asked for my name and I said, 'Hi, I'm Jeannie.' Then you said, 'Nice to meet you, Jenny. And I just let you call me Jenny for like two weeks."

Luka threw his head back in laughter. "Then Cathy corrected me, but I didn't stop. I wanted to be different, so I made it my nickname for you."

"And you've been calling me that since we were teenagers."

They were on a spread of white cloth near the edge of the field, watching the reflection of the orange sun on the still lake. Jeannie had suggested the idea of a picnic for them to unwind. They had packed the lunchboxes with pizza, fruits, and wine and set out in the late afternoon. It was Jeannie's sophomore year in college. Luka's, too. Given how tedious college life was, it took a while for them to finally make time for themselves after being apart for a week.

Finding out that she was pregnant had come as a major shock to Jeannie. She had passed out when the doctor announced it to her after a series of tests. Barely twenty years old, Jeannie still depended on her parents to survive. Her strict, Christian parents. The last few weeks had been nerve-wracking for her. Sooner or later, she had to tell her parents about the news.

Luka had taken the news better than she had expected. He was taken aback at first and was unsure if he was ready for the responsibility, but later on, he'd thawed out. They had spent hours talking and convincing themselves that they were going to figure it out. Jeannie was not sure about that, given that they were merely college students with no source of income, but she chose to remain optimistic—for her unborn baby's sake.

"And what if it's a boy?" Jeannie asked, tilting her head up. "What would we name him if it's a boy?"

Luka stared into space. "Gerard."

Jeannie's smile turned into a frown. "You really want him to get beat up, don't you?"

"Now you're exaggerating."

"You know what I mean," Jeannie said. "Anyway, one thing this conversation has taught us is that you are terrible at coming up with names, Luka."

Luka scoffed. "Well, I don't see you coming up with any names," Luka said. "Let's hear your suggestions, Miss Jeannie Miller."

"Hmm..." Jeannie sighed. "I'm thinking...Fiona, Adeline, Francesca...If it's a boy, then, Felix, Stephan, William, Harry."

"Great. Straight out of a princess book," Luka said. "Shouldn't we name our baby something that has meaning?"

"Oh, so the name Poppy has some meaning?" she asked.

"Yes, it does," Luka answered. "Or it will. You know what? I'm standing by Poppy, and no one will tell me otherwise."

Jeannie giggled. "We'll see about that."

They had been dating for five years, since they were seventeen. Luka was like Jeannie's other half. They did everything together, had great understanding of each other's minds and actions, and liked the same things. Luka always knew how to turn Jeannie's frown into a smile. She believed genuinely in her heart that he was her soulmate, and no one could tell her otherwise. Not even her parents.

They never said it out loud, but Jeannie knew they didn't approve of her relationship with Luka. For some reason, her mother never liked Luka. She always told Jeannie to be careful with him, because apparently, she didn't like his smile. Her mother always claimed Luka never smiled with his eyes, and she had a problem with it.

Jeannie's father, on the other hand, didn't want Jeannie dating at all. He hated the idea of her getting entangled with a man at a young age and was a firm believer in waiting till after college before dating a man—and preferably waiting till marriage before having sex.

Now, she was pregnant, with a man they didn't like, and out of wedlock. There was no way on God's green Earth that they were going to be receptive to the news.

"What are we going to do about my parents?" Jeannie asked. "We need to tell them, Luka. They need to know."

"I know," Luka mumbled. "You know they don't like me, right? They never say it, and they always force a smile when they see me, but I can tell. They haven't liked me since I was fourteen years old."

"Tell me about it," Jeannie groaned. "I have no idea why. What's there not to like?"

"That's what I'm saying!" Luka voiced.

Jeannie giggled and hugged him tightly. "We just have to find a way to make them see what I see. The perfect man for me. Trust me, my parents love me. I'm sure with time, they will understand. For now, we need to tell them somehow. I don't want them finding out on their own. It'll be better if we sit them down and tell them we want to move in together, and that we're having a baby. What do you think?"

Luka sighed and nodded. "I really think that's our only option at this point. More of the convincing has to come from me. I might not have a job right now, but I will get one soon, and I'll take care of you, Jeannie. I've already gone to the coffee shop by the school and I applied. They interviewed me and promised to call back. I'm positive I'll get the job. Just trust me."

Jeannie pecked him on the cheek. "I trust you, Luka."

"Thank you," Luka said, stroking her hair. "I love you, my Jenny."

Jeannie tightened her arms around him. "I love you, too, Luka. Always."

Chapter Two

It took a lot of willpower for Jeannie to open her eyes. She blinked slowly and repeatedly for a minute, trying to adjust her eyes to the bright light from her window. Still tired, Jeannie managed to drag herself off the bed and into the bathroom. She had to supervise work at the shop to get everything ready for the unveiling. Thankfully, most of the work was done, and all that was left were the final touches. She was still having a bit of a problem with the wiring for the electricity. Some of the floor tiles had cracked during the moving of the heavy equipment, and Jeannie had just noticed that the paint on the wall in the bathroom was peeling.

Other than that, everything was set. The chairs, tables, equipment...everything else. Jeannie noticed that her excitement had dwindled since the very first time she saw the shop. She had thought the period leading up to the unveiling would be very exciting for her, but to the contrary—she was numb and tired.

After a warm shower, she finally felt alive. She was in the middle of buttoning up her shirt when she recalled the events of the night before. Aaron and Luka had almost come to blows in her living room. It was all coming back to her, but still, she couldn't understand why all of that had happened. *What did Luka want? Do I even want to know why Luka came up from New York to Chickadee Cove to see me?*

The only reason Luka ever tracked her down was to gain access to her life so he could destroy it again. It was always the same, and yet she had fallen for it several times. But now, things were different. It had been two years since their divorce. There was no way Luka was coming back into her life—or her children's lives.

Jeannie scoffed. "No way…" she mumbled under her breath as she took out the chicken that was left in the oven from the night before. *At least I remembered to turn the oven off.*

But what was that dream, then? Of all the things she could have dreamt about—her children, Aaron, the shop…even Cathy—she had to dream of Luka. Of the time they were still in love.

Focus, Jeannie.

She had to get to the bakery. Luka was a distraction. They had so many memories together, but she'd spent the past two years getting over him. There was no way she was wavering now. Dressed and ready for the day, Jeannie stepped out of the house and made her way to the shop.

A few hours passed before she finally sat down. The contractors were busy in their respective corners, and she supervised their work before leaving them to it. The thought of Aaron had been at the back of her mind since she took her first breath of fresh air, but Jeannie found herself dodging those thoughts.

Why, Jeannie? Why?

Jeannie bit her fingernails, staring into space. It was

probably wrong to ask Aaron to leave, too. Why did she do it? Luka had no right to be there.

Jeannie felt butterflies in her stomach just thinking about him. The setting, the mood, Aaron's beautiful smile. It was the most romantic thing that had happened to her in years. If only Luka hadn't shown up to ruin it.

It didn't feel right asking Aaron to leave last night, especially recalling the look on his face right before he walked out the door. Aaron had looked disappointed. It hurt Jeannie to think she disappointed him.

Or perhaps she was overthinking it. Aaron would have understood that she was not in her right mind. It might have been the wine, Luka's presence, or both, but she didn't mean any harm when she had asked him to leave with Luka. She just wanted to be alone.

"Ma'am?"

Jeannie turned around.

"Yes?" she said to the electrician.

"I'm done with the repairs," he said. "Would you like to check them?"

"No." Jeannie shook her head. "I'm sure it's fine. Thank you."

"Alright. If you need anything, don't hesitate to call," he said, picking up his toolbox. "Have a nice day."

"You, too."

Jeannie's phone buzzed in her pocket. She pulled it out excitedly, expecting a call from Aaron, but instead she saw an unknown number displayed on the screen. Still hoping the call was from him, she accepted it and put the phone to her ear.

"Hello?"

"Jenny."

Jeannie groaned and hung up immediately. From the way things were looking, it seemed as though Luka was going to be trouble for her if she didn't take care of it fast.

I think I need Cathy's opinion. Seeing as Aaron hadn't called her all day long, Jeannie was starting to sense that he had taken offense at her actions. It was also possible that she was overreacting, but still...

It was best to call Cathy.

"What? Who came? What were you doing? Did something happen to Lily?"

Jeannie placed the phone away from her ear and shook her head. Trust Cathy to be dramatic about the entire thing. She had barely even told her half of what happened and she was already asking multiple questions.

"Would you please calm down?" Jeannie asked. "Let me start all over. Listen, alright?"

Jeannie heard Cathy gulp. "I'm listening."

"Good. Yesterday, I told you I had dinner with Aaron, right?"

"Right..."

"Well, it started off well. But I forgot to prep the chicken on time, so it was still in the oven when he arrived. We had some wine while we waited for the chicken, and then we started dancing. Then, Aaron kissed me, and—"

"He kissed you!"

Jeannie bit her lower lip to stifle a smile. "Stay focused, Cathy. That's not the point."

"Alright, fine. But we're not skipping past that. We'll come back to it later. Go on."

Jeannie took in a deep breath. "Cathy, he asked me to be his girlfriend with a beautiful ring and for a second, I thought I'd pass out from the excitement."

"Oh, how romantic," Cathy cooed. "Aaron is really romantic. I had no idea. So, what did you say?"

"I didn't have time to respond, Cathy. That's the thing. That's what I was trying to tell you. Luka showed up. He showed up and ruined the whole thing."

"What? Luka, as in...your ex-husband?"

"Yes," Jeannie groaned. "He showed up with bags and completely ruined the moment. You know what's worse, Cathy? I spaced out. I couldn't think. I was utterly flabbergasted by his presence."

"Well, what did he want?"

"I don't know," Jeannie answered, massaging her temple. "Honestly, I don't even want to know. Luka was threatening Aaron. He was asking him to get away from me, he shoved him, he was practically throwing a tantrum."

"My goodness. Didn't you tell him to leave?"

"I did."

"Good."

"But I also asked Aaron to leave, too."

There was a short pause on the other end. "You did what?"

"I know." Jeannie groaned again. "I wasn't thinking, Cathy. Then they started arguing and they were about to fight, and I panicked."

"Luka, I understand. But why would you ask Aaron to leave, Jeannie? One, he was there first, two, you like him, and three, he likes you."

Jeannie rose to her feet and paced. "That's what I'm saying, I don't know. Do you think he's angry? Is that why he hasn't called? I should call him, shouldn't I? I should probably have called him first thing this morning."

"You know what you should have done? Not sent him away."

"We've established that, now tell me what to do already," Jeannie asked, growing impatient.

"Well, what did Aaron say when he was leaving?"

"Nothing. He just took his jacket and walked out. He didn't say a word."

"Ouch."

"What?"

"That's bad."

"Why? Why is it bad?" Jeannie stammered.

"It means he's disappointed. He probably expected more from you."

Jeannie frowned. For some reason, she felt like she was on the verge of tears. "Oh, I knew it. I totally ruined it all."

"You know, seeing how this turned out, I don't think you're over Luka, Jeannie. At least not yet. It seems he still has some control over you."

"He doesn't, I assure you," Jeannie said. "It's probably just stress and lack of sleep for why I acted the way I did. But that's it. It's not Luka, I'm sure of it. Luka is my past. He's behind me."

"If you say so."

"Now, tell me what to do about Luka—I mean, Aaron. I want to call him, but I don't know what to say. What do you say to someone who is disappointed in you? How do you get them to forgive you?"

"First, get rid of the baggage, Jeannie. Luka is pushing his way back into your life and it upsets me."

"He's not back into my life."

"He is!" Cathy yelled. "Are you blind? He was in your house, with bags. He didn't come here to play around or get some fresh air. He came here for you. Now, whatever his plan is isn't your concern, like you rightly said, but it doesn't change the fact that he is here in Chickadee right now. Get rid of him. Ask him to go away. You need to stand your ground, Jeannie. Having Luka around is not good for you."

"You're speaking as if I want him around," Jeannie said. "It's not like I can tell Luka to go away and he would oblige."

"Not with that attitude he won't," Cathy said. "What happened to being firm? You can't face Aaron proudly and tell him you want to date him when your ex-husband is still lurking around."

Jeannie nodded slowly and took her seat. She recalled how the meeting between Aaron and Luka went. As far as meetings go, theirs was horrible. There was no way her relationship with Aaron would thrive with Luka around.

"Cathy, I'll take care of Luka later," Jeannie finally said. "Right now, Aaron is a major priority of mine. How do I fix this?"

"Call him!" Cathy answered.

"And say what?" Jeannie groaned. "You know what? I'll just call and apologize. I just hope he's not holding a grudge."

"Say whatever feels right," Cathy said. "But I need to go. I'll talk to you later, alright?"

"Talk to you later."

"Oh, and Jeannie? Don't ruin this."

Jeannie hung up and placed a call to Aaron. She held her breath as it rang. There was nothing in her mind to say, nothing at all, she just wanted to hear his voice. She knew that if she did, the conversation would figure itself out.

"Hi, you've reached Aaron Horn. Leave a message at the beep and I'll get back to you as soon as I can."

Jeannie hung up and dialed the number again. She had no idea what to say, hence voicemail was not an option. The phone rang the second time and, like before, she was directed to voicemail.

After about five tries, the calls started being directed to Aaron's voicemail without it even ringing. She drew in a shuddery breath, panicking.

He was avoiding her calls.

Was this it? Was this the end? Had she managed to ruin everything with her sheer stupidity? The more she thought about the incident, the more Jeannie cringed. He had tried to defend her from the ex-husband who had ruined her life, and she'd punished him for it. She felt like bursting into tears. Aaron might not have been just disappointed.

"Oh, come on. Pick up," Jeannie groaned, rising to her feet.

"Hi, you've reached Aaron Horn. Leave a message at the beep—"

Jeannie ended the call and squeezed the phone in her fist. Bombarding Aaron with calls was going to do more harm than good. She'd wronged him, so she had to take the bull by the horn.

Quickly, Jeannie placed a call to Cathy. She tapped her feet on the ground, listening to the phone ring. She spoke immediately when the dial tone stopped.

"Cathy, I need Aaron's address. As soon as possible, please."

Chapter Three

Once the text message containing Aaron's address dropped into Jeannie's phone, she practically sprinted out of the bakery. She went home first to put on more appropriate clothing; a pair of black jeans and a striped yellow and black t-shirt. She tied her hair up into a ponytail, so it didn't get in her face, then she slipped on a pair of sneakers and rushed out of the house again in minutes.

Her next stop was the pizza shop. What better way to apologize than with his favorite food? She picked up a medium pepperoni pizza and a bottle of white wine from the store nearby, then took a taxi directly to Aaron's home. The taxi came to a halt in front of a gated one-story building. The house had a nice green yard and shrubs that formed a perimeter inside the fence. Three different cars were parked out front. The building itself was white, with long pillars holding it up on two sides. It was big—bigger than she had expected it to be. If she had to make a guess, there were more than ten rooms in the house altogether.

Jeannie stared at the gate's intercom for a full minute before she finally pressed it. She had no inkling of what to expect. A couple of days ago, she had been warning Aaron about how pizza was not a healthy choice, but there she was, desperately using it to her advantage.

"Aaron?" Jeannie said softly. He had said hello through the intercom but remained silent after. "Aaron, aren't you going to let me in? I came here to apologize. I'm sorry for being a total weirdo. I'm sorry for embarrassing you like that. And for disappointing you."

A couple more seconds passed before the gate buzzed and opened slightly. Jeannie walked into the yard, paused, and took a deep breath before she continued walking again. The house was a good distance from the gate, so Jeannie walked down the path, admiring the beautiful yard as she went. She reached the front door and saw a doorbell, but as she was about to press it, the door creaked open.

"Hello," Jeannie blurted, trying to gather herself. She cleared her throat and smiled. "I didn't think you'd let me in."

"Honestly? I was contemplating it," Aaron said, standing by the door. "What are you doing here, Jeannie?"

"I came to see you," Jeannie answered. "I brought pizza and wine. You weren't answering my calls, so I thought I'd stop by instead."

Aaron remained silent. It was just as Jeannie had suspected. She had offended him, but he was staring at her with a placid face, making it difficult for Jeannie to tell what he was thinking.

"I am sorry, Aaron," she said. "I can tell that you're upset. I shouldn't have asked you to leave. In my defense, I wasn't thinking straight. But I truly am sorry."

Aaron sucked in a breath through his teeth and continued to stare at her. He obviously still wasn't convinced.

"Remember when you convinced me your name was Frank?" Jeannie asked, tilting her head to the side.

A feeling of relief washed over Jeannie's entire body when

Aaron's gaze softened. Finally, she got him to smile. Aaron sighed loudly before stepping to the side and gesturing for her to come in.

Jeannie stepped into the house, a relieved sigh slipping from her and a wide smile on her face. Half of the work was done. She took a moment to assess the vast hallway, noticing that the ceilings were high. The house looked bigger on the inside than it did from the outside.

Aaron shut the door after her and walked in front of her. She followed him promptly. Aaron led her into the living room and took his seat on the couch. He watched her walk into the room, too, and he didn't take his eyes off her until she sat down opposite him.

"You have a beautiful home, Aaron," Jeannie noted, breaking the awkward silence. "You seem to love the color white. A lot. Everything's white. It's neat and beautiful. I can't explain the calming effect your home is giving me right now."

"Thank you," Aaron answered.

The silence again. They were seated too far apart from each other for Jeannie's liking. Perhaps it was because of how vast the room was, and how much space was between them, but Jeannie would have preferred to meet at her place, where they would sit together in her living room or in her kitchen.

"Do you want to go to the kitchen counter instead?" Aaron asked, almost as if he had been reading her mind.

"Yes, please," she answered, stifling a smile.

They walked into another hallway and soon arrived in his kitchen. Jeannie set the pizza and the bottle down on the counter and sat on a high stool. It didn't seem like he used the kitchen at all. There were barely any pots or pans in sight, and his burners were spotless.

They sat next to each other this time at the kitchen counter. Aaron had his fingers interlocked and he sat directly facing the kitchen. Jeannie, on the other hand, turned her chair to face him. He was obviously still upset, and she had run out of ideas on how to apologize.

"Aaron, at least say something," Jeannie asked. "You haven't really talked to me since I arrived. I know you're upset, so let's talk about it."

"What do you want me to say, Jeannie?" he asked. "You're right to assume that I was embarrassed. I mean, who wouldn't be? We were in the middle of something I thought was important, but apparently, you didn't think so."

"No, that's not what happened, I promise," Jeannie said. "I admit that I was startled when I thought you were going to hit Luka, but that's why I asked you both to leave. I couldn't deal with the violence."

"Well, you could have asked Luka to leave, seeing as he was the one who interrupted us. But you asked me to leave first."

Jeannie sighed. "Aaron, I wasn't thinking straight. I'm sorry. I promise I didn't mean it that way. I wanted to be alone in that moment. Luka's presence completely disrupted my thinking process. I was scared at first because I thought something had happened to Lily. It just...all happened in the blink of an eye. Can you please forgive me? I'd like to think that you know me, Aaron. You know I wouldn't intentionally hurt your feelings."

Aaron squinted his eyes and turned to stare at her. He held her gaze for a few seconds before turning away. A half smile formed at the corner of his lips as he reached for the pizza box and threw the lid open. He took a piece out for himself, and then took another one and handed it to Jeannie.

"I thought you said pizza was bad for me?" Aaron asked, taking a bite.

"Oh, well. I knew it was the fastest way to get to your heart," Jeannie said.

"It really is. The sodium in this just shoots right into my heart. I wouldn't even see the heart attack coming."

Jeannie laughed at his remark. "Oh, you know what I mean. I'm glad it worked."

Aaron set his pizza down. "Can I ask you a question that's been bothering me since yesterday?"

Jeannie put her slice of pizza down, too. "Sure. You can ask me anything."

"Luka called you Jenny. Not Jeannie, Jenny. Why is that?"

Jeannie exhaled loudly. "It's a pointless story, to be honest. He refuses to stop, even though I've told him countless times to. It was sweet at first, that he had a nickname for me. But when he calls me Jenny now, I feel irritated."

"Ah, a nickname," Aaron mumbled. "Your divorce...it ended well? You both were on good terms when you signed the papers?"

"Absolutely not," she said. "I couldn't even look at him. It was so messy, Aaron. He refused to sign the paper for weeks. He didn't come to the court, he didn't come for the meetings to discuss the children, he didn't show up." Jeannie took in a deep breath. "When he came back the last time, and I told him there and then that I wanted a divorce, he left three days later. He didn't actually disappear, but he started to avoid me. It took a lot to get him to listen. My lawyers were on him every day. It took threats from the court to get him to sit down. He yelled, tried to manipulate me, he threatened me, he threw a tantrum. Regardless, I stood my ground and I made sure I saw it through till the end. Then, right after that, he disappeared. And now, he's back...again."

"Do you know what he wants this time?" Aaron asked. "I mean, it's different now, isn't it? You both aren't married anymore."

"It's way different now," Jeannie answered. "I'm not the Jeannie I used to be. I'm not the pushover that he once knew. If I could get through that divorce after holding on for so long, then there's nothing he can say to me now that can move me. Nothing at all. I don't know what he wants, and frankly, I'm not interested in finding out."

"You might not want to admit it, but you have to be curious." Aaron said, rubbing his chin.

Jeannie sighed. "I'm not sure why I have to deal with this baggage now. I don't want Luka's presence to affect what we have, Aaron. You and Cathy are the only ones I like to talk to. Besides my kids, that is."

Aaron chuckled. "I understand that, and I'm flattered. Thank you."

"You're welcome," Jeannie said. "And I'm sorry we didn't get to have our chicken like we were supposed to. We could go back to my place tonight, and I could maybe bake more chicken, so we can finish what we started. What do you think?"

"I'd like that, but I can't," Aaron explained. "Because of the time difference between us and China, I have a virtual meeting with some investors in Beijing at 9 p.m. It will be a long meeting, so I don't expect it to end till midnight."

"Oh," Jeannie managed to say. She bit her lower lip, hoping that her disappointment didn't show. "Well, I guess some other time then."

"Definitely," Aaron answered. "But trust me, I'm not pissed. It might seem childish, but it just hurt because you didn't pick me. I understand now that you wanted to be alone at that moment. I'm hoping whatever it is that your ex-husband wants to discuss with you isn't serious. Or—"

"Trust me, Aaron. I don't want to hear what he was to say," Jeannie said. "He has been calling me all day, but I just know that if I answer, I'll get a headache. I think I know what he wants, but I'm not giving it to him."

"A second chance?" Aaron asked.

"More like a hundredth chance," Jeannie scoffed. "It infuriates me to think that he came here for that reason. I cannot wrap my head around the idea that he had the audacity to come to Chickadee Cove to ask for another chance. It makes no sense. No one can be that oblivious."

"Well, hopefully, he's not here to cause any problems," Aaron said. "But I have to ask. It wasn't always like this with Luka, was it? I mean, it's either you didn't see the warning signs at first, or you chose to ignore it when you married him. Did he change? Or did you just get tired of his attitude?"

"Money changed him," Jeannie explained. "Luka wasn't always like this. Luka and I had been dating right from high school. We'd known each other since we were probably fourteen. We both got into the same college, and while in college I got pregnant. It was tough, getting my family to accept our child, but they eventually did. We got married and started to make plans for the baby. Luka was the perfect partner and father anyone could wish to have. He was there, he tried to make money for us, he listened. Thankfully, because of him, I didn't have to stop my program. Then one day, everything changed. Luka suddenly came into money by taking part in a TV game show. He won $500,000, and then I saw what money could really do to people. At first, the money made things easier. We got married, got a place together, and we were very comfortable. Then Luka discovered Vegas, where he thought he could double his money by betting and gambling. Luka dropped out of school, and instead of investing some of the money, he went on a spending spree. He became a serial cheat, slept out, partied nonstop, and flew all around the world, leaving me to care for our kids while still being a student."

"And you stayed with him?" Aaron asked. "After everything? For over fifteen years?"

"I was an idiot," Jeannie said. "You know what still baffles me? Two years after I gave birth to Mason, Luka reappeared and I took him back. My parents begged me to break up with

Luka, but I was desperate to make my marriage work, so instead of moving back to Maine after college, I moved to New York to be closer to him. I got my heart broken so many times, you cannot even imagine."

Aaron was silent for a while. "I think I understand why you kept going back to him. You weren't an idiot, you were being optimistic. 'This time he's changed.' 'He has seen his children, there's no way he'll abandon them again.' 'He said he'll do better, I just need to trust him.' I'm pretty sure you said these sentences to yourself repeatedly until you believed them."

Jeannie inhaled deeply. "Oh, well, I learned my lesson. Right now, I'm just trying to be happy. I just want to open my shop and spend the rest of my life in peace. I think my heart deserves some peace and quiet."

Aaron reached for her hand and squeezed it. "You deserve it. You raised beautiful, respectful children who are thriving in the world right now. You didn't need Luka for that, and you don't need him for anything now."

Jeannie fiddled with her fingers. "I don't want him around my children at all, Aaron. They might be adults now, but what he did to—"

The sound of Aaron's ringtone interrupted them both. Aaron reached for his phone in his back pocket and pulled it out.

"Jeannie, please excuse me. I have to take this," he said.

"It's alright, go ahead."

Aaron turned to the side and began a conversation. Jeannie picked up a few words and was able to decode that Aaron's meeting had been moved to earlier that evening. Whilst still on the call, Aaron rose to his feet and scurried around the room. After a few minutes, Aaron returned with an apologetic look on his face.

"I know," Jeannie said before he could say anything. "I

understand. Go do what you have to do. I'll see you tomorrow."

"No, wait," Aaron said. "Wait for me. The meeting has been moved to 7 p.m., but I have to get to the mill first to gather some documents. I'll just have the meeting there and come right back. I should be back by 10."

"Aaron, I can come back tomorrow. I'm sure you will be tired from the meeting."

"Wait for me," Aaron said again. "Please. I don't want to come back to an empty house."

Jeannie felt a tingle run down her spine. "Alright," she said, almost in a whisper. "I'll wait."

"Thank you." Aaron smiled. "I'll buy one more box of pizza on my way back."

"No. Do not buy any more pizza. We barely touched this one," Jeannie said.

"Alright, fine." Aaron chuckled. "We'll have some wine when I get back then. I'll show you my wine cellar. I have an extensive collection of premium antique wines."

Jeannie felt herself smile. "I would like to see that."

"I'll like to show you," he said, "when I get back."

Jeannie rose from the seat and escorted Aaron to the door. She waved goodbye to him and watched him drive out of the gate. When he was out of her sight, Jeannie returned to the living room and sank into the soft sofa.

Chapter Four

Jeannie woke up to the echo of silence. The first thing she saw when her eyes were fully open was the high, coffered ceiling of the room she was in. If she recalled correctly, the ceiling in her cozy bedroom was as conventional as they came.

Jeannie sat up quickly and scanned the unfamiliar room. It looked like a hotel room, but then, she couldn't have been in one. The last place she remembered being in was Aaron's house. He had left for work in the evening, and she had stayed. The last thing she remembered was falling asleep on the sofa cushion.

"Did he carry me?" she mumbled, rubbing her eyes.

For a moment, Jeannie contemplated lying back down on the bed. It felt as if she were sleeping on clouds. The duvet was nice and fluffy, and so was the bed. Given the picture on the wall, the awards neatly placed on a rack, and the slightly open wardrobe by the right filled with men's t-shirts, Jeannie could guess that she was in Aaron's bedroom.

The only way she could have gotten there was if he'd carried her, or if she'd sleepwalked. It couldn't have been the latter, as she had never sleepwalked before in her life. Which left only one option.

Reluctantly, Jeannie dragged herself to her feet and stretched her entire body. She had not had such a good night's sleep in days...weeks, even. If it wasn't for the aroma of pancakes that was seeping into the room, Jeannie would have returned to bed. She strolled to the kitchen quietly, so she could get a peek at Aaron before he saw her.

"Jeannie?" Aaron called out to her. "Is that you?"

Jeannie scoffed, baffled. She hurriedly walked out of the hallway and stood in front of the kitchen counter with her arms akimbo.

"How'd you know I was coming?" she asked, tilting her head to the side. "I'm pretty sure I didn't make a sound."

"Yes, you did." Aaron smiled. He had a spatula in his hand and a small spoon in his mouth. He had a shirt on that was only buttoned on the last button. Beneath it, he had on a black tank top and a pair of white shorts. "Good morning, Jeannie. Breakfast?"

Jeannie's cheeks flushed bright red. "I'd like some, thank you."

"Coming right up."

"First I need to ask..." Jeannie continued. "When did you get back home? How did I get in your bed? Where did you sleep?"

Aaron smiled and turned around to face the pan on the burner. "Interesting."

"What is?" Jeannie asked.

"I just...you asked me the time I got back home. I can't explain it, but I liked how it sounded. Almost as if we lived together."

Jeannie was having great difficulty controlling the fluttering in her heart. She placed a hand on her chest and massaged it. If she didn't get it under control soon, her entire face was going to turn bright red, not just her cheeks.

"You didn't answer my questions," she said.

"Right." Aaron cleared his throat. "I got back in at about... 12 a.m. When I walked into the living room, you were sleeping soundly on the sofa. I didn't want to wake you, but I didn't want you to spend the night in the living room. So I carried you to the bed and tucked you in. Don't worry, I slept in the guest room."

Jeannie scoffed. "I'm not worried. But you should have put me in the guest room."

Aaron shook his head and turned back around. "My bed is way better."

"I agree," Jeannie blurted. "I haven't slept that well in weeks."

Aaron set the plate down on the table. "Well, you are welcome any time to come sleep in my bed."

"Thank you." Jeannie giggled. "And thank you for not waking me. I really had a nice rest. I feel really refreshed now and ready to take on the world."

"I'm glad. Do you have any plans for the day?"

Jeannie picked up her fork and dug into her food. "I'm just now realizing that I didn't supervise the contractors yesterday when they were working on the shop. I have to go back and check if they did a good job."

"Why didn't you?"

"I was distracted."

"By what?"

Jeannie gave him a knowing look. "What do you think? A certain someone was avoiding my calls and my text messages."

Aaron dropped his head. "I told you, I was throwing a tantrum."

"Still, because of you, I wasn't focused at the shop. I have a couple of people I need to interview first, but I haven't had time to fix a meeting with them. There are still some finishing touches that need to be done, but the shop should be ready for launch in about a week."

"That's impressive, Jeannie," Aaron said. "I recall how you started it all. When you arrived at the mill, trying to buy materials by yourself and all. Now, you're done with all the preparations, and soon, you'll be living your dream. I'm impressed."

"Thank you." Jeannie beamed. "And point of correction, we started it all *together*. Or are you forgetting that you were the first person to work on the shop? If it wasn't for you, I honestly don't think I would have made this much progress in such a short time. Thank you."

"You're welcome." Aaron smiled.

They spent most of the morning together talking about the shop and exchanging ideas for the opening event. Jeannie knew that once she started baking, her mood was going to change completely. It was all she wanted to do, and she was so glad she was getting to do it before she became too old or frail to do anything.

"Let me drop you at home?" Aaron offered.

They were standing in the yard. Jeannie had completely lost track of time, and it was almost noon. As hard as it was to do, she needed to leave Aaron alone to work and return to her own shop.

"Aaron, go back to work," Jeannie said. "I can get home myself."

"I know that, I just want to drop you," Aaron insisted.

"No," Jeannie said. "I'll take a cab. I prefer to."

"Would you drive my car instead?"

"No," Jeannie said, laughing. "See you later, Aaron."

They hugged briefly before Jeannie made her way out. She was in a much better mood than she was when she first walked into his home the night before. Jeannie was thankful for the spontaneous decision to go in search for Aaron. It felt as though they had become closer overnight.

Jeannie figured that she'd use the time to get her shop in order and start on that new path. It was hard for her to trust people, but things were different with Aaron.

The smile on Jeannie's face quickly turned to a frown when she arrived at her house to find Luka standing outside. He had his back against the wall, his arms crossed, and his foot was up against the wall. Jeannie contemplated staying in the cab till he went away, but she had no idea how long he would wait there for her, and she had things to do.

"Thank you," she said to the driver with a sigh before getting out of the vehicle.

Just ignore him and maybe he'll go away.

Jeannie worked up the confidence before approaching the driveway. She didn't smile and crossed her arms over her chest as she strolled to her front door. Luka was quick to notice her. He stuffed his phone in his pocket and took a step forward.

"Where have you been? I've been waiting here for you for over two hours," he said. "Did you not come home last night?"

Jeannie paused in her tracks. Luka was making it really difficult to ignore him.

"Luka, what is this?" she asked him. "What do you think you're doing?"

"What do you mean? I asked you a question. Where have you been?"

"Why are you here?" she asked. "You know what? I don't even want to know. I don't understand you, Luka. We have been divorced for two years. This isn't the scenario where you disappear and then come back and beg, expecting to continue where you left off. No, this isn't it. This is the new reality. Where I am free from you, and I have a life here in Chickadee Cove. I owe you nothing, Luka. My children are grown, and they have lives of their own. You might think that Emily, Mason, Kelly, and Lily are the things tying us together, but you are wrong. Nothing in this world connects us."

"Not even the memories we shared together?" Luka asked. "Jeannie, you were my first love."

"I couldn't care less about that," Jeannie answered, trying not to laugh in his face. "I don't care about anything you have to say. If I could turn back time, it would be only so I didn't have to meet you. The only good thing I ever got from knowing you are my children. That's all. Leave me alone, Luka. You have your many girlfriends in different corners of America. Go to them. You can go to Patricia, the one you slept with when I was in labor. Or Kelly. The one I never understood, because I could never wrap my head around the fact that you could sleep with someone that bore the same name as your second daughter."

"They were all mistakes," Luka said. "You know this very well. You know I never know what I'm doing when I'm drunk. I don't even remember sleeping with these ladies. That's how drunk I was."

"Sure. Always blame it on something. That's the Luka way," Jeannie said. "I don't care. I stopped caring, get it through your thick head. I have a life here. A good one. I am happy, and I would like to keep it that way. I have a good thing going on for me, and the last thing I want is you ruining it."

"Jeannie, please list—"

"I won't," she said. "I'm not listening to you. Luka, don't you know what you are? You are a liar and a cheat. I won't waste my time on you. Leave me alone. If you keep on coming to me, I will go to the police and file a restraining order against you. I promise."

"I just want to—"

"I will say it again if you weren't listening," Jeannie said sternly. She lifted her finger and pointed it at him. "Leave me alone, Luka. Go away from here. Get out of my life. If you refuse, I will have you arrested for stalking."

"Jenny—"

"Don't call me that!" Jeannie shouted at him. "My name is Jeannie. Jeannie Miller. My parents named me Jeannie, not Jenny. I don't want your stupid nickname, it irks me. You are like a thorn in my side, Luka. Please. I am begging you to go away."

With that, Jeannie shoved him out of the way. She walked quickly to her door, dug out her key, and jammed it into the keyhole. Luka was still standing behind her and she knew it, but she didn't look back. She had to be strict with her orders. That was the only way to get it through to him. Luka was never one to listen. He always knew how to manipulate his way into people's minds. Giving him an audience wasn't a good idea. The best course of action was to turn him away before he got into her head.

"I have cancer."

Jeannie froze. Perhaps she didn't hear him correctly. Or perhaps she did, but it was one of his tactics again. Still, she reluctantly turned around to stare at him.

"I don't have a lot of time left," he said with a quivering voice. His eyes were watery and his face had turned red. "And I'm scared, Jeannie. I'm horrified. I know who I am...or who I was, and I know you have doubts about me. But I came all this way because you are the only family I have left in this world. I have no one. Just you and the kids. That's why I tried to make amends with Lily. I'm dying, Jeannie."

Jeannie could not utter a word. Luka had his ways of manipulation, but she had never seen him this vulnerable before. Her mouth failed to form words and when she stood there, quiet for too long, Luka nodded and walked away.

Her mind going completely blank was starting to become a habit.

Chapter Five

The smell of damp air oozed through the window and filled the room. Jeannie laid down facing her familiar ceiling with her hands on her stomach, like she had frozen on the spot.

She hated how she was feeling. Just the day before, she had been ranting about her hatred for the man she used to call her husband to anyone willing to listen, and now, in what was practically the blink of an eye, she was feeling sorry and sad for him. Their conversation leading up to his announcement and the sudden change in his demeanor kept replaying in her head. She'd said a lot of things, most of which were incredibly hurtful.

It was unbelievable and totally absurd that it only took the news of him dying to soften something inside her. Luka was not a good person. He was a mighty good example of how to be a bad father, and he had hurt Jeannie in more ways than one. But there she was, lying wide awake in bed feeling sorry for him.

Cancer was not a joke. Jeannie wouldn't even wish it on

her worst enemy, who in this case just happened to be Luka. Perhaps it was God punishing him for his numerous sins.

There was still a chance in all of this that Luka was lying. That was what he knew how to do, and he did it well. It was this same ability, coupled with his manipulation skills, that had managed to fool Jeannie all those years. What if this was another ploy of his to get back into her life and ruin it again? Things were finally starting to look up for her. Even after the divorce, even after gaining her freedom from him, after two years, things were just starting to improve. What if Luka was back to ruin it?

But for what reason? They were not together anymore, and there was no way on Earth that she was going to ever make the mistake of seeing him again, much less marry him again. The mere thought of being romantically involved with Luka caused a rash of prickly goose bumps to appear. That chapter was closed. Forever. Luka knew this. He was aware that she was never going to forgive him. Why would he lie about his health?

Still, Jeannie couldn't aptly categorize what she was feeling for Luka in that moment. She was sorry for him, that much was obvious. She pitied him, too. Cancer hurt. Sooner or later, he was going to need all the help he could get. One thing Luka was right about was the fact that he didn't have anyone. His parents were dead, he had no siblings, and no relative that he was close to. At least, none living. Her children were the only ones who could carry on his last name. But three of them were girls, and the only man, Mason, chose to bear Jeannie's last name.

If he truly was sick, then it made sense that he had come all the way here to find her. Even though things had ended badly between them, they had children together. They had known each other for more than half of their lives. Perhaps he didn't want to get back together with her. Seeing how scared he looked, Jeannie could only guess that Luka was seeking a companion in his troubled times.

That would explain why Lily had been nice and receptive toward him. Even though she hardly knew the kind of man her father was, Jeannie couldn't expect her daughter to turn away Luka when he was dying. Maybe that was the reason Lily didn't listen when she had asked her to send Luka away.

Jeannie groaned and rolled over onto her stomach. After staying awake for most of the night, she still could not come up with a course of action, given her recent discovery. What was she going to do? Surely, she couldn't maintain her abrasive demeanor toward him. Not when the man didn't have long to live. But having him around wasn't a good idea, either. Jeannie had a life now, and there was a man in her life, too. Luka's presence was going to cause too many issues.

Sending him away was not an option, either. Jeannie didn't have the heart to. There had to be a way around it without it upsetting Luka, his health, or her new life.

Still tired from the lack of good sleep, Jeannie managed to rise to her feet and walk over to the kitchen. She poured herself a cup of hot coffee and sat at the counter with her phone in hand. Emily, Mason, and Kelly needed to know. It would be better if they heard it from her, since they tended to ignore Luka's calls. Speaking to them could also help Jeannie find a way around the issue.

With that in mind, Jeannie placed a conference call to Emily, Mason, Kelly, and Lily.

Why does Lily never answer my calls?

A feeling of déjà vu sent slight chills down Jeannie's body. It was an all too familiar setting, except for the fact that when they had talked about Luka in the past, they were always together in the living room, not on FaceTime.

Usually, when Jeannie had to sit her children down for anything concerning Luka, she had to mentally prepare herself for the reactions. It got more and more difficult to convince them that their father was back for good, that he had left on a business trip, or that he had retired from his work abroad and was back home. Of course, Emily, Mason, and Kelly never believed her. They would throw tantrums and ask that he leave, since he was so good at doing that.

One of Luka's sins that hit the children pretty hard happened when Mason was still in middle school. News had circulated that Luka had slept with their English teacher, Kelly. Jeannie knew it was true, and she had confirmed it through numerous dirty texts on Luka's phone, but she had tried to convince Mason otherwise. He knew the truth, hence he never believed her. After the incident, Luka disappeared again, and when the noise had long died down, he returned. That was about it for the father-son relationship between Luka and Mason.

"She's on a movie set, Mason," Emily answered. "She has barely posted anything on social media in two days, so I'm guessing she's occupied. I left her a message, and she said she'd call when she can."

"I haven't spoken to Lily in days," Kelly said. "When she calls you, Emily, please tell her to call me, too."

"I will," Emily answered and yawned. "Hey, Mom. You're awfully quiet. Is something wrong?"

Jeannie snapped out of her thoughts. "I'm sorry. I was just thinking about something, that's all. Is everything alright with you guys? Emily, Mason...how's work? Kelly, isn't it time for your honeymoon to end? You're currently on a yacht, aren't you?"

"Yes, mummy." Emily giggled. "I'm pretty sure my

honeymoon has ended, and I'm just...living at this point. Are you sad that I haven't come to visit you? Is that it? Do you want to come here instead? It's beautiful out here, Mom."

"Maybe some other time," Jeannie said with a smile. "I have to open my shop, remember?"

"Right. Well, just tell me when you want to come visit and I'll make sure to put everything in place," Kelly said.

"I will, honey. Thank you."

"So, why did you call, Mom?" Mason asked. "Is something wrong? Do you need anything?"

Jeannie shook her head. "I don't. I actually called to tell you three about something very important. I'm sure Lily already knows about it, but it would be unfair of me to keep this information all to myself. I figured you all need to know. That's why I decided to call you all."

"Oh, it sounds serious. I'm scared," Mason teased. "What could possibly be the issue that you're too scared to tell us?"

Jeannie took in a deep breath. "It's your father."

"And what about him?" Mason asked. "Don't tell me he did something to Lily. Did Lily call you to say something?"

"No, it's not about Lily," Jeannie answered. "Your father is here in Chickadee Cove. He came to me."

"What?" Emily replied. "What does he want?"

"He has cancer. At least, that's what he said. Luka claims he doesn't have that much time to live."

There was a pause on all their ends for a few seconds. Jeannie fiddled with her finger. Before the call, she had been unable to predict how they would react. The one thing she was sure of was that they didn't care about where Luka was or what he was up to. The three of them had stopped caring for their father long ago. Jeannie wasn't sure the news of his illness was going to have any effect on them. But again, he was still their father, so she couldn't tell.

"That's not good," Mason said first, breaking the silence.

"Does he look sick, Mom? Is his hair starting to fall out? What stage is the cancer? What kind of cancer is it?"

"He didn't say," Jeannie answered. "I was a bit harsh to him when he came to me. At first, I didn't give him a chance to speak. I thought he was playing his usual game, where he comes out of nowhere asking to be part of our lives again. I thought that was what it was. So when he came asking to speak to me, I didn't let him get a word in. He was able to tell me he had cancer before he walked off. I would have called his bluff, but I saw the look on his face, you guys. I don't think he's putting on a show."

"That's terrible," Kelly said. "Cancer is a terrible thing. I hope he beats it and gets better soon. Did he come to you for money? Is that the problem, Mom? Did he run out?"

"No, that's not it," Jeannie answered. "He didn't come for money."

"Then he came all the way to Chickadee Cove to only inform you about his illness?" Emily asked. "That doesn't make any sense."

"He came with bags," Jeannie explained. "Big bags. My guess is, he's not leaving anytime soon."

"He's not what?" Mason chimed in. "I don't understand, Mom. Please don't tell me he's living at your house."

"What? Of course not. When he arrived, he came here with bags asking to speak to me. But at the time, I was with Aaron, and things looked as though they were about to get messy, so I asked them to leave. I don't know where Luka is staying right now, but he is somewhere around town, I'm sure of it."

"Why, though?" Mason asked. "I mean, obviously, I feel bad that he has cancer, but he has no business with you, Mom. Why would he have bags? And why is he in Chickadee Cove? What does he want with you?"

"I have no idea," Jeannie answered. "But things are different now."

The three of them murmured through the phone. Mason went as far as groaning, and Emily kept saying no.

"I cringe when I hear you say things like that, Mom," Kelly said. "Things are different now. Have you not learned your lesson?"

"It's not like that," Jeannie explained. "It's not the same this time. Luka and I are not going down that path anymore, so don't even think about it. What I mean is, unlike before when Luka came back to reconnect with us, this time it's different. We cannot ever be a family again, so that's not what he's looking for."

"How do you know?" Emily asked. "You know he's not after us, Mom. He might claim that he wants to reconnect with us and be a family again, but it's not us he always comes back to. It's you. He uses us to get to you. Right now, he's trying to use Lily to get to you. I hope you see that."

"It's not like that," Jeannie reiterated. "Come on, you guys. How can a man dying of cancer be thinking about reuniting with his ex-wife?"

"Then what does he want?" Mason asked. "You haven't told us what he really wants yet. He has cancer? Really sad thing, but he shouldn't be in Chickadee Cove. He should be in a hospital getting treatment so he can beat it as fast as possible."

Was Jeannie the only one seeing the entire situation from a different perspective? From what she could gather from their conversation, her children and Cathy were on the same page. They all wanted Luka gone. She, on the other hand, didn't want to make any rash decisions and end up regretting it.

"So, what do I do?" she asked. "I can't just turn him away."

"Uh, yes, you can," Mason answered. "He was able to walk

out of our life and stay out for many years. I'm thinking it's your turn to do that now. Mom, there should be no reason for you both to be together anymore."

"I agree," Emily said. "I still can't even understand why he thought coming to you was a good idea."

"You shouldn't even be giving him an audience, Mom. That's how he gets to you. You're not a doctor, or a nurse. What help could you possibly give him?"

"I can't just turn him away," Jeannie said. "Not when he's dying."

"He's not dying," Mason said. "If he can still walk on two legs without any help, then the cancer hasn't gotten to him yet. The best you can do is ask him to see a doctor. He has the money to buy all the care he needs."

"Mason, I'm sure Luka is scared enough as it is. That's why he came to me. He probably just wants someone to confide in."

"And why do you care?" Mason groaned. "We're not doing this again. Send him on his way. Let him go back to Lily, since she's the only one who seems to tolerate him."

"When people hear that you have been meeting with your ex-husband, they'll make assumptions," Emily said. "What about Aaron? Don't you care about how he'll feel if he sees you getting vulnerable like this again?"

"I'm not getting vulnerable," Jeannie said. "I'm trying to be human. I'm trying to put myself in his shoes. We all know that Luka has made terrible mistakes in the past, but we are the only family he has. We might not want to try and become one again, but we can at least support him through this difficult time."

"We can," Kelly said, "but from afar. Not there in Chickadee Cove. You cannot live with him. People will start talking. I'm pretty sure Aaron will ask questions, too. And what happens when Luka finally beats cancer? Do you really think he'll just disappear?"

"And what if he cannot beat it?" Jeannie asked.

"Then he did all he could," Emily said. "But that is on him, Mom. Not you. That's what he gets for not taking care of his family. There is nothing we can give him. Nothing at all. It's shameless of him to even expect anything from us."

"I have to go now, Mom," Mason said. "Don't ruin the good things you have going for you for a man that will disappear once he's better. You do know that when he doesn't see the use for you anymore, he'll leave? Like he has always done? It's time for you to pay him back for all of that. Tell him to leave Chickadee Cove, find a good hospital in New York, Washington, or wherever, and get treated. Luka is never going to change. I'll talk to you later."

With that, Mason ended his part of the conference call, leaving Emily and Kelly still on the call with Jeannie.

"Mom, I have to go, too," Emily said. "But I stand by what Mason said. Luka is a grown man who can take care of himself or hire someone to do so. It hasn't even been that long since he came to you, and you already look stressed. Cut ties now."

"I knew she should have gotten a restraining order against him during the divorce process," Kelly said. "If you did, then all of this wouldn't be repeating itself. Bye, Mom. Talk to you later."

Jeannie waved them both goodbye and dropped the phone to the counter. She dropped her head onto her palm and grabbed a chunk of her hair.

"What do I do?" she groaned.

<h1>Chapter Six</h1>

Deep down in her heart, where she had buried logical thinking, Jeannie knew her children were right. It was sad that Luka was ill, but letting him have access to her life so easily, after trying for years to get him out, made all of their efforts seem like a joke. They had every right to be doubtful, and if Jeannie was honest with herself, she shouldn't be feeling sorry for Luka.

Past experiences with Luka had molded the image of him that the children had in their minds. Such that when they heard their father had returned, they immediately imagined that he wanted to ruin their lives again. Even with the cancer, their opinion about him was unwavering. They still wanted him out of their lives.

Jeannie couldn't blame them. After all he did to them, how could Luka expect any remorse from her? It was shameless of him to do so, but desperation was also a terrible driving force. Luka was in need of companionship, but he had ruined his chances and burned bridges with his children.

"You don't seem to be paying attention," Aaron said,

keeping his eye on the laptop. "You have barely gone through one application."

Aaron's voice snapped her back to reality. They were seated in a small office inside the bakery going through applications for her job openings at the shop. Jeannie needed to be scheduling interviews already, but she had barely sorted through the applications yet. When she informed Aaron, he volunteered to help. Given that he was an employer himself, he knew what exactly to look for.

"Oh, I was just...sorry," Jeannie said. "I was a bit distracted."

Aaron closed his laptop and faced her. "By what?" he asked.

"Just something random. Are you done reviewing those applications?" Jeannie inquired, changing the subject. "I'm almost done with mine."

For whatever reason, Jeannie reckoned it was safer to not get Aaron involved regarding Luka anymore. She didn't know how he would take the news of Luka's illness, and it would break her heart if he also had an issue with her being indecisive. It was best to wait till she knew what she wanted to do before involving Aaron.

"Yes, I sent the impressive ones to your email. If you want, I can send the ones I didn't think were good enough to invite for interviews so you can skim through, just to be sure."

"Oh, no. I trust your judgment." Jeannie smiled. "When I'm done with my own half, I'll draft out an email for the successful ones. I need to be done with this before the opening event."

"Would you like me to draft the email?" Aaron asked. "It'll be easier for you to just review it and send."

Jeannie paused and met his gaze. "Aaron, you have already done too much. I can handle the rest. Seriously, I'll do it. It won't be a problem at all."

"It's not a problem for me, either," Aaron said. "But if you want to handle it, no problem. Is there anything else you would like some help with?"

Jeannie scanned the office. "No, nothing at all. I think everything else is pretty much set. I just need to fill in the vacancies at the store and find out if I can drag my children from their busy lives to come for the opening event."

Aaron chuckled and leaned back in the chair. "Well, given that Kelly is just getting back to work from the honeymoon, Mason is in the middle of a season, and Emily teaches at a college in the middle of a semester, the only child of yours that might be able to show up is Lily."

Jeannie set the papers aside. "Lily can't even come."

"Why not?" Aaron asked. "You know Lily is the only one I haven't spoken to. From the look of things, she's the one I have to impress the most."

"Aaron, even I barely speak to her these days," Jeannie said. "I should be glad that she is chasing her dreams and having a mind of her own, but honestly, I am not. I still want her living under my roof even though she's already eighteen. She's not matured enough for the world. But she asked me to trust her, so that's what I'm doing. Trusting her. I'm sure if she needs anything, she'll call me."

Aaron leaned forward. "I'm sorry if I'm prying, but I do have another personal question."

Jeannie nodded. "Okay, I'm listening."

"You once said that your children don't have a good relationship with their father. They don't talk to him?"

"They practically hate him at this point," Jeannie said. "And it's his fault."

"Because he kept leaving?"

"Because he made it so obvious that he was a terrible dad," Jeannie said. "When the kids—Emily, Mason, and Kelly— were still in high school, there was this joke that the other kids always said to them. If the teacher or someone random inquired about their father, someone would randomly say, 'Oh, he went to buy some milk, he'll be back soon.' It hurt the kids a lot that most of their friends and classmates knew."

Aaron's eyebrows furrowed. "How did...how did they find out?"

"Well, Luka slept with one of the teachers at the school," Jeannie explained. "That was years before the bullying started. Her name was Kelly Princeton. I can never forget it because it never made sense to me. One of the kids in Mason's class that lived across the street from Kelly saw Luka coming out of her apartment one morning on his way to school. So the rumors started, and then the principal found out, and Kelly didn't even try to deny it."

"You wanted her to deny it?"

Jeannie nodded. "Pretty pathetic of me, but I did. For Mason's sake. If she had denied it, even if I knew, then perhaps the children would have been saved the embarrassment. They were too young to be hearing all of that. But then she came apologizing, saying it was a mistake...that she didn't mean for it to happen. It just blew everything out of proportion. I think that was the icing on the cake. Luka had done a lot of things prior to that, but that incident was one they never forgot."

"So, to date, they don't speak to him?"

Jeannie nodded. "They don't."

"Then how did he find you?" Aaron asked. "I mean, who could he have asked to get your location if you all weren't in touch with him? Is Cathy in touch with him?"

Jeannie scratched the back of her head. "It's not Cathy. It's Lily."

Aaron raised his eyebrows. "Lily is in touch with him? You knew?"

"I found out when I went to California to visit her,"

Jeannie revealed. "I didn't tell you. Luka was with Lily when I got there. I'm sure she gave him my address."

"So, Lily is on good terms with her father?"

"She is," Jeannie said. "She wasn't born during all of this, and Luka left again when she was very young, so she doesn't have a lot of bad memories about him. Only the good ones. It doesn't matter what we tell her, she was brainwashed by her father. That's what he's good at. Getting in people's heads."

"Then he shouldn't be around you, Jeannie, right? If he is so good at getting into people's heads?" Aaron asked.

"That was in the past," Jeannie stuttered. "There's no reason for him to try and get in my head now. We're done."

"That's what you keep saying, but I can tell that you're keeping something from me. And I'm pretty sure it has to do with Luka," Aaron said.

"What? No," Jeannie lied. "I have it under control, Aaron. Trust me. I'm not the Jeannie I used to be. I'm more logical than I am emotional now. I think the air in Chickadee Cove is good for me."

"I would really like to meet the former Jeannie and ask her a couple of questions," Aaron said. "What was she thinking? Was she so in love with Luka? Why did she accept him back if he cheated on her once before..."

"Twice before, that I know of," Jeannie corrected. "I'm sure there were more women. He couldn't have been alone for all those years. Especially when he disappeared for fifteen years. I'm sure there were more of them."

Aaron stared at Jeannie with his mouth ajar. "Jeannie—"

"I know." Jeannie smiled and dropped her head. "But thinking about it now, it wasn't love, Aaron. I stopped loving Luka over a decade ago."

"Then what was it? What made you always forgive him?"

"The children," Jeannie answered. "He knew how to use them, and he knew how to use our past. What we had. I was trying to make sure that my children had a father figure in the home, like the other kids their age. We lived in this neighborhood where everyone was married, maybe not happily, but they were together. Husband, wife, children. My house was different. It was me and my four kids. I didn't even have time to date. I couldn't because I was legally married, and it would be cheating. So whenever he came back begging, I succumbed, hoping that we could have that model family."

"But he always left."

"Always," Jeannie whispered. "I hate this, honestly. I hate having to talk about Luka. I've seen him, I've been thinking about him, talking about him. I hate it. When we had the divorce, I never wanted anything to do with him ever again."

"Have you seen him since that night?" Aaron asked. "You need to tell him, Jeannie. It doesn't have to be hostile. Just make sure he gets your point. Explain it to him, that you don't want anything to do with him anymore. Frankly, I'm curious as to what he wants with you. A part of me is convinced that he is looking for another chance. You might think you're over it and you're over him, but you can never tell how the mind works. He might say something that appeals to you, and then you're trapped again, unable to wiggle him off. You have to stand your ground."

"I know." Jeannie nodded. "Now, can we please talk about something else? I don't want to talk about Luka anymore."

"Your wish is my command," Aaron said, leaning back. "Have dinner with me tomorrow night."

The butterflies were back again.

"Where?"

"It's a surprise."

"Oh, I like surprises." She beamed.

Aaron lifted one eyebrow. "Do you? Do you really? 'Cos when your ex-husband showed up at your door, you—"

"Okay, fine. Maybe I'm not a fan of surprises," Jeannie said and rolled her eyes. "I'd like to have dinner with you."

"Good," Aaron said, visibly pleased. "And I know this is a shameless ask, but...if you eventually talk to Luka, tell him about me. I don't know how you would want to introduce me, given that I'm practically sitting on a fence, but...I just want him to know that you have me in your life."

Jeannie bit her lower lip to stifle her smile. "I will."

"Thank you."

They spent the rest of the day drafting the emails to send out for the interviews. Jeannie felt bad about withholding information from Aaron, but she convinced herself that it was for the best. Sooner or later, he was going to find out, but Jeannie preferred that he did so later. All she wanted in that moment was to enjoy Aaron's company without Luka interrupting it in any way.

Chapter Seven

J eannie's cheeks hurt from smiling so hard. That morning, she had woken up with a headache that refused to go away. Going about her activities for the day had been torture, and then the evening finally came, and she was really contemplating cancelling her dinner plans with Aaron.

But apparently, happiness did cure headaches. She had been staring at the dress in her hand for more than five minutes. Jeannie had thought it was going to be a casual evening. She had picked out a nice, knee-length dress with short sleeves to wear for the date. But Aaron had other plans. He had sent her a dress; a beautiful, expensive one at that.

Excited to thank him, Jeannie set the dress down carefully on the couch and picked up her phone. She placed a call to Aaron and stood in the middle of the room as it rang, still staring at the dress.

"Hello? Aaron?" Jeannie said.

"I'm guessing you got the dress."

Jeannie bit her lower lip. "I did."

"Oh, thank God. I wasn't sure it was going to be ready in time for the evening. Do you like it? Have you tried it on?"

"I love it. I haven't tried it on, but I know it'll fit me," she answered, smiling sheepishly. "How'd you guess my size?"

"I have my ways," Aaron answered.

"Do your 'ways' involve Cathy?"

"They do," Aaron answered.

Jeannie laughed and ran her hands down the dress. "Thank you, Aaron. You really didn't have to, but it's nice to know that you're thinking about me. I had a bad headache this morning that was literarily torturing me, but it has just vanished all of a sudden."

"A headache?" Aaron asked. "Do you get them often?"

"Occasionally," she answered. "It's usually not a big deal, but lately, it's getting constant and more intense."

"Did you take any pills?"

"I think I developed a tolerance for the pills," Jeannie said, still admiring the dress. "If it persists, I'd have to go to the hospital, right?"

"I was about to say the same thing," Aaron replied. "I'll check back tomorrow and if you still have a headache when you wake up, I'll take you to see my doctor."

"Alright, thank you," Jeannie said. "Thank you for the dress."

"You don't have to keep thanking me, Jeannie," Aaron said. "I'll see you at seven?"

"I'll be ready at seven."

Jeannie picked up the dress and took it into the room to get ready for the evening. The fact that it was all new for her was both sad and exciting at the same time. Jeannie was forty-seven years old, and this was the first time since she was a teenager that she was receiving a thoughtful gift from a man, that she was that excited for a date with someone she cared about, that a man had her concerns in mind and was worried about her.

The best part of all of this was that Aaron didn't even have to try. She liked him so much that even the littlest things he did were enough. It was obvious that he cared for her, and he not only told her, he showed her, too. Jeannie had still not figured out how she was going to do the same for him. The man had everything he wanted, and she had little to give. Sometimes, she wondered why he was interested in someone like her in the first place when he could easily have someone better. Someone with their life together.

Jeannie's phone rang and she rushed out of the bedroom to the living room to answer. She hoped that it was Cathy, given that her friend had promised to help her get ready, but she hadn't arrived yet. To her surprise, it was Kelly.

"Hi, baby." Jeannie beamed after accepting the call.

"Hi, Mom!" Kelly said. "I heard you're going on a date."

Jeannie's jaw dropped. "How in the world did you find out?"

"Mason told me," Kelly answered. "Aaron told him. Apparently, Aaron called Mason to ask what your favorite color was."

Jeannie glanced at her bedroom door. She scoffed and shook her head. "And Mason told him blue? Really? Blue?"

"Blue? What did Aaron get you?"

"A blue dress," Jeannie said. "It's beautiful, so I have no complaints. But my favorite color is actually purple. Not blue."

"I thought it was red."

Jeannie squinted her eyes. "Do you both even know me at all? You can't even guess my favorite color."

"That's unimportant stuff," Kelly said. "Now, back to the reason I called. What are you doing with your hair? Your makeup?"

"I don't know, Kelly," Jeannie groaned. "Cathy was supposed to come over to help me get ready, but she isn't here yet."

"Well, call her," Kelly said. "When you call her, call me back, alright?"

"Why?"

"I need to see what you look like before you leave," Kelly said. "You need to take this date seriously. I heard Aaron met Luka, too. You told Emily, but you didn't tell me. We don't like how things are starting to play out. Luka is getting too involved with you, Mom. If Aaron gets uncomfortable with his presence, he'll leave. Do you want that?"

"What? Why would he leave? He knows the relationship between Luka and me. There's nothing there. He has nothing to be worried about."

"Does he also know that you act all tough about moving on, but you always take Luka back?"

"That's different." Jeannie took in a deep breath and shut her eyes. "I'm not talking about Luka tonight, Kelly. Please. It is a Luka-free night. I have a date to prepare for."

"An important one. You need to look your best, Mom. Aaron needs to fall in love with you all over again. That way, he won't think about leaving."

Jeannie snorted. "Let me call Cathy, Kelly. She's running late."

"Call me back!"

Kelly had succeeded in turning up the tension. What if Aaron was truly having second thoughts, given that Luka was now present in her life again? Jeannie couldn't have it. Aaron was the one good thing that had happened to her in a long time. She couldn't risk losing him.

Jeannie placed a call to Cathy twice, but she wasn't answering. She was on her own for the date, and that alone was a recipe for disaster. She had no idea what to do with her hair or makeup.

So she placed a call to Kelly again.

"Hi, honey. You might need to give me a virtual class on how to apply some makeup on my face, alright?"

It was about thirty minutes to seven o'clock when Jeannie had finally finished with her look. She and Kelly had argued so much over the phone, her throat hurt. But they had finally agreed on a look. A simple dinner look. Thankfully, Cathy had left her makeup bag with Jeannie after the first date she had with Aaron, hence Jeannie had some options to choose from.

After wiping off four different lipsticks from her lips, they finally decided on a nice pink lip gloss lined with a brown pencil. The first one she wiped off was a red lipstick that did not match the blue color of the dress at all. But Kelly thought otherwise. She claimed the red was intense and different. Jeannie didn't agree. Then they tried purple, her favorite color, and they both agreed that it was just not it. Then there was brown, and it made Jeannie look like she was suffering from an illness, and then orange, which she had no comment on.

The pink was perfect—simple.

Doing her eyebrows was a hassle that Jeannie had not been mentally prepared for. She groaned so much and was close to losing her temper when she finally got it right. Kelly had screamed in excitement that the arches were symmetrical.

She had gone for a blue eyeshadow and blended at the edges with black tint. Then she lined her eyes with a black pencil, curled her eyelashes, and used a mascara to make them thicker.

For her hair, the only thing Jeannie could do well was a high bun. Since there was no one to help with any other style, they agreed on it. Jeannie used a band to gather her hair in a high ponytail, then she wrapped it around into a bun.

The dress...

If she weren't wearing any mascara, Jeannie would have cried. But ruining her makeup was not an option. It was an ankle-length, sky blue fitted dress with a long slit on the side. Tiny stones were used to adorn it, making the dress shimmer. Jeannie was not the curviest, but the dress really accentuated her figure. It had elbow-length sleeves and a low V-neck.

To go with the dress, Jeannie paired it with a small, silver clutch bag and silhouette heels. She couldn't stop staring in the mirror.

"Mom, I wish I could take a picture of you right now," Kelly said. "But I'm hoping Aaron will take some and send them to us."

"I'll take many pictures, not to worry."

"Do you know where he's taking you?"

Jeannie shook her head. "Not yet."

The sound of the doorbell startled Jeannie. "He's here," she said, panicking. "He's here. He's here."

"Bye, Mom! Have fun!" Kelly said and ended the call.

Jeannie took one last long look at herself in the mirror before scurrying out of the bedroom. She paused at the door, took in a deep breath, and opened it with a bright smile on her face.

"Hello, Jenny."

Her smile changed to a frown in a millisecond. "Oh, no, not you."

"Ouch," Luka said, stepping into the room. He took one long look at her with his mouth slightly ajar. "Goodness. You never looked this breathtaking when we were married."

"That's because I was miserable," Jeannie said. She could feel her headache coming back. "Look, Luka. I don't have time for whatever this is. I don't have time for you."

"We need to talk, Jeannie," Luka said. "I know you hate me right now. But we really need to talk."

Jeannie mellowed, recalling his condition. "I know this is a hard time for you, Luka. But I am going somewhere in about twenty minutes. I don't have time today."

"I'm not leaving until we talk," Luka said, taking a seat. "It's either you sit and hear me out, or your new plaything comes in and sees us together. Remember how he tried to punch me the last time he saw me?"

Jeannie groaned. The sooner she got rid of Luka, the better. She only had to listen and make a decision based on her own best interest.

"Fine," she said, sitting across from him. "You have ten minutes. Talk fast. I'm serious."

Luka raised both hands in the air. "That's all I need." He cleared his throat. "First off, Jenny—"

"We're not doing this, Luka," Jeannie said, cutting him off. "Get serious. I've told you countless times not to call me that."

"Why?" Luka smirked. "It still has the same effect on you?"

"I will leave, Luka," Jeannie threatened.

"Fine, sorry," he mumbled. "First off...Jeannie, I want to apologize to you. I did so many horrible things to you and our family, especially to you. When people say money is the root of every evil, they are not lying. I can admit that money changed me. It changed my life. If I could go back to twenty-six years ago, when we were regular college students, in love, happy...I would. I would change everything in the blink of an eye. I'm so sorry for my mistakes, Jeannie."

Jeannie didn't want to get emotional thinking about the past. It would ruin her mood, and her mascara.

"Apology accepted," she said, sniffing deeply. "Is that it?"

Luka wiped the corners of his eyes. "Of course not. I'm

dying, Jeannie. I don't know when, but it's happening. I have nothing to lose at this point."

Jeannie sighed and dropped her head. "How did you tell Lily?"

"Lily? I haven't told her yet. You're the only one I've told," he answered.

Jeannie's eyebrows furrowed. "Then why did she let you stay?"

"Because she understands and forgives me, Jeannie," Luka said. "That's all I'm asking for."

Jeannie scoffed. "She doesn't know what you did to her, that's why. That's all you ask? You're speaking as if understanding and forgiveness are trivial things. For you, it costs a fortune to acquire from me. I will never understand you, Luka."

"Even if I want to be better?" Luka said. "I know it's probably late for us, but I don't want to give up. I want a chance to change, Jeannie. To make amends. I can do it."

Jeannie squinted her eyes. "What do you want from me exactly, Luka? I don't understand."

Luka shifted to the edge of his seat. "I want us, Jeannie. I want us to start afresh. I want the love we once shared. Remember how we were in college? How much love we had for each other? How we used to go on picnic dates at our favorite spot. We know everything there is to know about each other. We started this journey together, and we have four kids to show for it. Let's finish it. Let's end this journey together."

Jeannie found it difficult to close her mouth. "There's no way..." she muttered, flabbergasted. "You're telling me this is the reason you came all the way to Chickadee Cove? To ask for another chance? Are you serious, Luka? You can't be serious."

"I've never been this serious in my entire life, Jeannie."

Jeannie rose to her feet. "You are insane."

Luka rose to his feet, too. "Jeannie, like I said, I have

nothing to lose. Nothing at all. I have closed every other chapter in my life. I don't drink anymore, I don't smoke, I don't party, I don't gamble…I wasted years of my life doing it. At least, if I'm dying, let me do it with the only person I have ever actually loved in my lifetime."

"Luka, I can't do this right now," Jeannie stammered. "I honestly didn't think you had the audacity to ask me for something like this, but apparently, you have nothing to lose."

"Think about Lily, Jeannie."

"You will not play that card with me, Luka. I know you, I know about all your tactics. I'm not falling for it."

"I'm going to tell her I have cancer, Jeannie. You know how fragile Lily is. It'll be better if we did it together. I don't want to break her heart again. I know I was stupid to leave for so long, but if I tell her that I'm dying, she'll be heartbroken."

Jeannie's heart sank. He was right about Lily. She didn't take bad news well. Jeannie had hoped that they had crossed that bridge, but Luka still hadn't told her about his condition.

"Lily wants us to be a family again," Luka continued. "That's her only wish. I want it, too. I want to grant her wish before I eventually pass away. Let me do this for my daughter, Jeannie. You have nothing to lose. Soon, I'll die, and you can move on with your life. I just don't want to go with regrets."

"You should have thought of that before you decided to disappear from our lives," Jeannie said. "If you really cared about your family like you claim, why did you treat us like a second option then? Like we were nothing to you?"

"I was young and very foolish. All I wanted to do was make more money for you and for our children. But I didn't make adequate plans with my life. Help me, Jeannie. Please. We're not young anymore. Why go in search for something new when we can build on what we already have?"

Jeannie glanced at the clock on the wall. "Luka, I say this from my heart. I am sorry you're going through this, but I really am not interested in fixing what we had. The best I can do for you right now is support you. We can be friends. I'm not comfortable with it, but it's the best I can do for you."

"Jeannie—"

"Luka, you really need to go," Jeannie said. "We'll talk some other time."

Luka stuffed his hands in his pockets and sighed. "Alright. I won't interrupt your date. I'll leave you. Have fun tonight, but please think about what I said. Please."

"Fine," Jeannie answered.

Chapter Eight

Why go in search for something new when we can build on what we already have?

"Are you angry that I was late?"

Jeannie had been so distracted by her thoughts that she didn't realize they had arrived at the venue. It was a terrible idea to give Luka an audience when she knew she had a date that evening. Seeing Luka brought back memories Jeannie had buried deep within her heart, and old habits that she had tried so hard to get rid of. One of which was her tendency to think "what if?" whenever Luka came back.

"Jeannie?" Aaron called her softly and took her hand. "What is wrong? Do you still have a headache?"

Jeannie jumped at his touch. "Um, yes," she blurted. It was best to blame her distraction on her headache, else she'd start stuttering and Aaron would be able to tell something was wrong.

"Do you want to go home?" Aaron asked. "I could order takeout and we'll just...maybe watch a movie or something?"

"No, no," Jeannie said, sitting up. "I don't want to go back home. I want to have dinner with you."

Aaron smiled. "I didn't tell you something about this dinner that I should have."

"What is it?"

"We are sort of...on a double date," Aaron said, massaging his nape.

Jeannie tilted her head to stare at his face. "With who? Please don't tell me it's Isabel."

"What? No," Aaron said. "Of course not. It's with a good friend of mine. He heard I was having dinner at his brother-in-law's Chinese restaurant, and he asked to join us. His name is Charlie Dukes. He's a senator here in Maine."

"Wait, Chinese restaurant?" Jeannie said, raising her eyebrows. "Cathy said there was a really popular one that was always booked. She had been trying to get in for like a month. Is this it?"

"Probably," Aaron answered. "It was a friend of mine—"

"Wait, did you say senator?" Jeannie cut him off. "Like... we're having dinner with a senator?"

"A state senator," Aaron said.

Jeannie was not discouraged.

"A senator nonetheless," she replied.

"And his wife," Aaron added.

Jeannie's jaw dropped. "Oh my goodness."

"I wanted it to be a surprise, then I thought about it, and it suddenly did not make any sense for it to be a surprise. It should have been a warning, actually, but I wasn't thinking straight. I'm sorry."

Jeannie giggled. "It's fine, Aaron. I've never been on a double date."

Aaron lifted his eyebrows. "You've never been on a double date? How's that possible—oh, wait...of course."

"Yeah..." Jeannie whispered.

"Are you sure you're fine with this?" he asked. "I don't want you to be uncomfortable."

Given that Jeannie was not fully present, the idea of a double date was great. That way, she could listen to other people talk. If it was just her and Aaron, he was going to find out something was off with her. Jeannie didn't want to give Aaron a reason to worry.

"I'm completely fine with this surprise, Aaron Horn," Jeannie answered. "It's not every day I get to meet a U.S. state senator."

Aaron got out of the car first and scurried over to Jeannie's side. He opened the door for her and took her hand. Jeannie thanked him and took her time to adjust his blue tie. She had been so distracted during the ride that she had not noticed how nice Aaron looked that evening. He matched her, with a blue and black suit and a glossy, blatantly expensive pair of shoes.

"You look beautiful tonight, Jeannie," Aaron said quietly. "I said it before when I picked you up, but I don't think you heard me."

Or she was too distracted...

"Thank you, Aaron," she answered. "You look amazing, too. I've said this before, and I'll say it again. You clean up pretty nicely. Who knew Frank the carpenter looked this dashing in a suit?"

Aaron chuckled and took her hand. The restaurant was a one-story building that stood alone in a huge compound. They had to pass through a large gate, and then into a beautiful yard with beautiful flowers and a beautiful, huge water fountain right in the middle. The sound of the falling water was soothing to listen to.

"Now I know why it's difficult to get a reservation here," Jeannie said.

The building itself was painted red with Chinese writing used to decorate the exterior. Even the name of the place was written in Chinese.

"Aaron Horn, please," Aaron announced to the young lady at reception.

She typed on her computer for a few seconds before lifting her head with a smile on her face. "This way to your table, please."

The first thing that caught Jeannie's attention was the huge chandelier hanging down from the ceiling. It was the only major source of light for the entire room. The walls were painted black, and the light bounced off it creating a dim, tranquil scene. Jeannie liked it. There were only a few people in there, even though the restaurant was always fully booked.

"The Dukes are here already," Aaron whispered to her.

Jeannie tightened her grip on Aaron's hand as they approached their table. There was a lanky man wearing a pair of glasses and a woman with Southeast Asian features at the table. They rose to their feet with smiles on their faces as Aaron and Jeannie approached.

"Aaron Horn. You are a hard man to sit down with."

Hard man to sit down with? She saw him every day.

"Good evening, Charlie," Aaron greeted him with a hug. "Good evening, Evelina."

Evelina reached for Aaron and pecked him on the cheek. "Hello, Aaron. It's nice to see you again. Who do we have here?"

Jeannie held her breath. "Good evening," was all she managed to say.

"This is Jeannie Miller," Aaron introduced her. "Jeannie, this is Senator Dukes, and his wife, Evelina Dukes."

Jeannie stretched forth her hand and shook Charlie's. "It's a pleasure to meet you, senator. You too, Mrs. Dukes."

"Likewise," Charlie said with a smile. "When Aaron said he had a dinner date and he wanted to make a reservation here, I didn't actually think he would bring a lady. It has been a long time since I've seen him hold hands with one. You must be special to him."

"Come on now, Charlie. We just got here. Don't make her uncomfortable," Aaron said. He placed his hand on the small of Jeannie's back and guided her to her seat, allowing her take a seat first.

They were seated at a round, communal table, the kind with an inner serving tray that slowly rotated. Jeannie sat quietly, listening to Charlie fill Aaron in on the details of his new business. It was easy to tell that the reason he requested the double date was to talk to Aaron about business. Jeannie didn't mind. She wasn't used to settings like this, and it was nice having the experience for the first time.

Besides, the food was an easy distraction from her troubles. It was delicious. Jeannie and Evelina made small talk as they ate. Evelina had a son and two daughters. She barely got to see them, hence she was always lonely. Her son was a resident doctor and her first daughter just got married.

"I have a daughter who just got married, too," Jeannie said. "I cried at her wedding."

"Oh, I cried like a child, Jeannie," Evelina said. "I had to be excused from the church. I couldn't control myself. She's in Tokyo now, with her husband. They are doing well. They are thinking of relocating to America soon. Her husband wants to expand his business, so once he finalizes all of that, I'll have my daughter back. Well, partially."

"Do they have any kids?" Jeannie asked.

Evelina shook her head. "None," she answered. "My youngest daughter, Caroline, she's twenty. It hurts me to say this, but that girl is a mess."

Jeannie set her chopsticks down and met Evelina's gaze. "Are all youngest daughters that way? Because mine is a mess, too."

They both laughed quietly so they didn't interrupt the men's conversation.

"I don't even know where she is right now," Evelina said. "Last I checked, she was in Dublin. Two weeks ago, she was in Seattle. She calls once in a while to inform us that she's alive but then disappears from the face of the Earth for another month. Charlie had to put a bodyguard on her tail. He's watching her for us."

"I wish I could afford a bodyguard," Jeannie said, shaking her head. "But even if I could afford one, Lily would throw the biggest tantrum if she found out I had someone following her."

"How old is she?"

"Eighteen," Jeannie said.

Evelina gasped. "I take it you don't sleep at night?"

"Barely," Jeannie answered. "That girl is the cause of my sleepless nights. She wants to be a model."

"Ah, well if she has your features, then I understand why. Is she all alone?"

Jeannie nodded. "We used to be together in New York. Then Lily wanted to follow that path and become a model. No matter how much I objected to it, she stuck with it. She's determined, I'll give her that. When she decided and moved out, I figured it was time to move on, too. That's when I moved to Maine. I grew up here, and I missed it."

"I understand," Evelina said. "I grew up here, too, and I can't imagine myself leaving."

"Sometimes I wish I'd never left," Jeannie said. "I wonder what my life would have turned out to be if I had just stayed in Maine."

Evelina smiled. "Do you have anything you do here? Or did your children ask you not to work anymore?"

"Oh, I'm opening a bakery downtown. I haven't set the date yet, but it's soon. That was how I met Aaron, actually. He came through for me when I really needed help. I joke about it, saying to myself that he was sent to me to compensate for the misery I had to endure."

"So, he's like, God-sent to you?" Evelina asked with a smile.

Jeannie glanced at him and nodded. "Yeah. But don't tell him or it'll get in his head."

"What are you both whispering about?" Charlie asked.

"Should we have been listening to you bore us with your lecture about money and architecture?"

Aaron reached for Jeannie's hand under the table and squeezed it. They met each other's gazes and smiled before turning away.

"Oh, I forgot to mention," Charlie said. "You look very pretty tonight, Miss Miller. The both of you look like an actual couple. You know how hard it is to get Aaron to wear a suit?"

"Just Jeannie, Senator Dukes," she corrected him.

"Just Charlie, Jeannie," he answered.

Jeannie smiled in response. "So, it seems like you've known Aaron for quite a while. Might I ask how you both met?"

Charlie dabbed the corner of his mouth with a napkin. "Oh, I was one of the first persons Aaron met when he first arrived here in Maine. He seemed so quiet and serious, until he started talking. Aaron here is a very good friend of mine. One I wouldn't trade for anything."

"You flatter me, Charlie," Aaron said.

The rest of the night was filled with more talking, laughter, and a lot of jokes. Jeannie had not laughed that hard in a long time. She had assumed the senator and his wife would be a stuck-up serious couple, but they were not. They talked to Jeannie like they had known her for ages.

At the end of the night, Jeannie was tired, but she had a

smile on her face the entire ride home. Aaron barely let go of her hand for the duration of the night, but she wasn't complaining. He played with her fingers, caressed her thumb... anything except letting her hand go.

"I had a lot of fun tonight, Aaron," Jeannie said. "Thank you."

"Anytime," Aaron said. "Jeannie, have you met with Luka?"

Jeannie's heart skipped a beat. "What? Why?"

"I'm just asking," Aaron said. "You don't know what he wants yet or why he's here. I just want to know if there is any development."

"No, none at all," Jeannie answered, averting his gaze.

Aaron arched his eyebrows. "Are you sure? I mean, isn't it weird he hasn't approached you since that evening?"

Jeannie shrugged her shoulders. She placed a kiss on Aaron's lips and went in for a hug. "Goodnight, Aaron. Thank you again. I'll see you tomorrow."

"Goodnight," Aaron said, rubbing her back.

Jeannie waited for him to drive off before walking into the house. She could tell that he had just let the issue of Luka go. He wasn't convinced.

Chapter Nine

It felt like her head was going to implode. Jeannie flung two aspirins in her mouth and pushed them down with an entire glass of water. Her head felt like an oven, and she had no idea why. She hadn't drank that much the night before.

Recalling the events of the night caused a smile to form on Jeannie's tired face. She made a mental note to call Aaron and thank him again. The night was one she was not going to forget in a hurry. She had met awesome, influential people, drank expensive wine, had delicious Chinese food, and laughed like she was at a comedy show.

It made her wonder if that would have been her normal life if she had married someone who actually cared. If she had a husband who took her on dates, who bought her flowers and thoughtful gifts...would she still be in awe of such lovely evenings?

Jeannie's phone rang and she didn't need to check the caller ID to know who it was. She groaned and threw the phone on the table before crashing on the couch. Luka had been calling her nonstop since she woke up that morning. The man was skilled, she had to admit. The way he ruined things for her needed to be studied.

Jeannie sat up abruptly. What if he was suddenly sick? What if he was having an attack, or the cancer was starting to cause him pain and she was ignoring his call, leaving him to die a slow and painful death? It would be her fault.

With that in mind, Jeannie sought out her phone and accepted the call.

"Hello?" she panted. "What is it, Luka? Is something wrong?"

"Hey, Jeannie. I just thought to call you and make sure you got home safely last night."

"Oh, for heaven's sake," she muttered, ended the call, and flung the phone away again. She should have known. If Luka was truly in pain, he would have called an ambulance, not her.

But what was she going to do about Lily? Thinking about it now, it was going to be a problem. She wondered how Lily would react to the news that her father was dying. As much as Jeannie hated to admit it, the girl wasn't stable.

There was a high probability that she was going to blame Jeannie for Luka's death. Lily wanted them to be a family again, as selfish as it sounded. Of course, Jeannie was never going to allow that to happen, and Lily didn't think of anyone else but herself sometimes. It scared Jeannie to think that Luka could use it to his advantage. That he could use her daughter against her.

Jeannie groaned and picked up her phone from the table. Perhaps this was her punishment for being stupid for decades. If only she had listened to her parents. To think that they told her to come home after Luka left the first time, but she said no and moved to New York with him. There were so many decisions in her past that Jeannie deeply regretted. But there was no changing the past. There was only planning for the future. She wasn't getting any younger; hence, all the choices she made had to be practical and logical.

Jeannie placed a call to Emily, hoping to find her available for a talk. She needed to talk to someone about Lily. She paced as the phone rang.

"Hello, baby?" said Jeannie. "It's Mom."

"Hi, Mom," Emily answered with a cracked voice.

"I'm sorry, did I wake you?" she asked. "I can call at another time."

"No, it's fine. I'm already awake," Emily said. "Are you calling to tell me about your date with Aaron? Did it go well?"

"You knew, too?"

"Of course. Aaron texted me. How was it?"

"It was wonderful. One of the best nights of my life," Jeannie said. "But that's not why I'm calling, baby. It's about Lily."

"What about Lily this time?"

"I tried to call her yesterday, but she texted me that she'd call me back. She hasn't called me back."

Emily groaned. "Oh, mother. Are you really worried about Lily not calling still? After what happened when you freaked out and went to New York to visit her? She'll call on her own time."

"I know. I'm sorry, that wasn't what I wanted to talk to you about. Did any of you tell Lily about her father's condition?"

"I don't think so," Emily answered. "I haven't spoken to Lily all week. Mason is in the middle of a season, and Lily gets on Kelly's last nerve, so they barely speak to each other."

Jeannie sighed in relief. "That's good."

"She doesn't know, does she?"

"She doesn't. Luka didn't tell her. He wants me to tell her, because he knows she'll have a mental breakdown, and I'm pretty sure he doesn't want to handle it."

"Oh, she will freak for sure," Emily said. "I think she actually prefers him to you, Mom."

"You don't think I know that?" Jeannie asked. "Why do you think I'm worried about telling her? The girl doesn't even know who her father really is, but he has sweet talked her into liking him, and now, he wants me to do the dirty work for him."

"Ignore it, Mom. Please. How many times do we have to tell you? Leave Luka alone."

"Don't you think if I could, I would have?" Jeannie asked. "You're asking me to turn a sick man away."

"So? He has money. He can take care of himself. Tell him to book a hospital room and get all the care he needs. Mom, you do not owe him anything. Let him tell Lily about his condition, too. Don't get involved. Just wait, and Lily will come running back into your arms when she realizes she'll lose him."

"I just—"

"What did you tell him, Mom?" Emily asked.

Jeannie sat down on the arm of the chair. "He wanted us to be a family again. That's why he came."

"What! Oh my goodness. I wish I was there. What did you tell him, Mom? Tell me exactly what you told him."

"I told him that he was insane and there was no way I was ever listening to him."

"Good."

"But I also told him we could be friends."

"Oh no, mother. What in the world does that mean? Why? How do you survive in this world if you are so soft? Did he care about you when you were in labor all by yourself, giving birth to Lily? How could he have cared? He was busy cheating on you with another woman. Did he care when he was the cause of the bullying we had to endure in school? Did he care? Now he's back, and you want to be friends?"

"He's sick, Emily."

"Mom, what is the matter with you? Why are you saying two different things? I'm not listening to this. I can't. Call me when you have told him off. Till then, I'm not listening to the excuses you're making for him. I will be extremely angry with you if Luka ruins things for you again. I won't speak to you anymore."

"Emily, come on—"

Before Jeannie could get another word in, Emily hung up the phone.

"I'm not making excuses," Jeannie said into the phone. "I'm just trying to be human."

Was it hard for her to see things the way her children saw them? Jeannie didn't like Luka, but she couldn't tell him to go away. Her conscience was never going to let her be. Did they really think she wasn't trying? She couldn't help how she felt.

It was late in the morning before Jeannie got out of bed again. She hoped to God that the person who rang her doorbell was anyone other than Luka. He was the cause of her stress, and she really did not need to see his face.

She opened the front door and a sigh slipped from her lips.

"Hi, Jeannie."

Instinctively, Jeannie threw herself at Aaron, falling on his chest and wrapping her arms around his waist. She sighed again, noticing that her headache had eased a bit as she saw him. Apparently, happiness didn't cure her headache the day before. It was Aaron.

"You work better than aspirin," Jeannie mumbled.

"Aspirin? What does that mean?" Aaron asked, patting her back. "Do you still have a headache?"

Jeannie nodded lazily.

"Alright, let's make that trip to the hospital," Aaron said. "It'll be quick."

Jeannie took him by the hand and pulled him gently into the house. "We can go some other time. I see you brought food. I am starving," she said, eying the bag of takeout in his hand. "What did you bring?"

Aaron set the bag on the table and sat down. "Mexican. I didn't know if you liked it, but I figured that if you didn't, we'd order something else. I tried to call you, but you weren't answering your phone. Were you asleep?"

Jeannie walked over to the other side of the counter and sat. She played with the bag, contemplating if it was a good idea to tell Aaron about everything.

"Jeannie?"

Jeannie glanced at him. "It's nothing. I'm fine, Luka. I was just tired from all the fun yesterday and I slept."

Aaron stared at her with a concerned expression on his face. One she couldn't understand. He stared at her as if he were waiting for something.

"Do you want me to get some plates?" Jeannie asked.

"You called me Luka, Jeannie," he said, biting the inside of his cheek. "I did not expect it to hurt the way it did. Were you thinking about Luka? How could you be thinking about someone you claim you haven't seen in days?"

"What?" Jeannie asked, trying to think back to what she said.

"It's fine," Aaron said, walking into the kitchen. He grabbed some plates and forks and returned to the counter.

"Luka, I am so"—Jeannie swallowed—"Aaron, I am so sorry. You're right, I was thinking about Luka before you came, but it's not what you think...or, I don't know what you're thinking, but it's definitely not anything you're imagining."

"You don't want to know what I'm imagining, Jeannie," Aaron said, plating the food. "It's okay. It's fine."

"No, it's not. It's not fine at all," Jeannie said, approaching him. "I was distracted."

"You've been distracted ever since he came here that day, Jeannie. You haven't been yourself and you're lying to me. I don't like it when I'm lied to, especially by you. I trust you enough to tell you everything about myself, and I have invested my emotions in you, Jeannie. Anything you do will hurt me, that's how much I care about you. But you keep lying to me. I've been waiting for you to tell me what Luka wants when you're ready, but you refuse to admit that you've met him. What did he say that you can't tell me?"

Jeannie paused to exhale. "He has cancer," she whispered. "It's something I could have told you, but I was tired of talking about Luka all the time."

Aaron's gaze softened. "He has cancer? You're sure?"

Jeannie nodded. "Well, that's what he says. I don't even know what to do anymore. He is scared, that's why he came to me. He has no one else to turn to for support. My kids...Emily is mad at me because I won't turn him away. I'm sure she'll tell Mason, too, and he'll get angry. But I believe Luka is dying, Aaron."

Aaron dropped his head. He was silent for a couple of seconds.

"I'm sorry I didn't tell you."

"It's fine," Aaron answered. "But what does he want with you? No offense, but if he truly is sick, he needs a hospital. He didn't need to move across the country to be here."

Jeannie fiddled with her fingers. "He just wants a friend till he recovers from it."

"A friend?" Aaron asked. "Who is that? You? Does that make any sense to you, Jeannie? You heard what you just said, right? The man who practically made your life a living hell wants to be friends with you, and you agreed?"

"What was I supposed to do? Turn him away?"

"Yes!" Aaron answered. "He needs to be in a hospital. Not here. Not with you. Have you forgiven him so easily?"

"Of course not. But how can I hold a grudge against a dying man?"

"How are you so sure he's dying?"

"That's what he said."

"And you believed him?"

"What reason does he have to lie about this?"

Aaron mellowed. He took Jeannie's hands into his and locked eyes with her. "Jeannie, as tragic as it may sound, it is not your problem. Don't get involved with him. He is your ex-husband for a reason."

Jeannie yanked her hand away from his grasp. "You all don't understand. I'm not trying to go back to Luka or mend our relationship. I'm just saying he is sick, and he has nobody."

"So, you want to take care of him?"

"That's not what I'm saying, either."

"Then what are you saying? What do you want to do for Luka? What is your aim? What do you want, Jeannie?"

Jeannie felt tears sting her eyes. "You're being selfish and cold, Aaron."

Aaron slapped his palm to his forehead and paced the room. "I'm being selfish? What are we, Jeannie? This thing we're doing, what is it? Wait, I know what it is to me. What is it to you?"

"That's not what we're talking about," Jeannie said and crossed her arms. "We're talking about the fact that you refuse to see beyond your own interest. Do you think I want Luka around me?"

"You have a choice," he said. "You're divorced. You are not

tied to him, or did you forget? No one is obligating you to be by his side in his fight."

"We are tied," she retorted. "We're tied by our children and our past. As much as I hate Luka as a husband, we were friends first. Before money changed him. It's cruel of you to ask me to ignore him and chase him away. I hate the man, but I'm not heartless."

Aaron brought both hands to his hips and nodded. "You know what? I think I see why Luka found it so easy to come back into your life."

"What's that supposed to mean?" Jeannie asked with a quivering voice and at the verge of tears.

Aaron picked up his jacket. "Bye, Jeannie."

With that, he walked out of the house without glancing back. Jeannie's heart was racing with hard, pounding thumps. She stood there waiting for him to return, but the door stayed shut.

He was gone.

Chapter Ten

Two days later...

Jeannie sat in the bathtub with her knees to her chest as the warm water slapped her skin. It was time to go to the hospital to complain about the headaches. Nothing was working for it anymore. She slept with a raging headache, and woke up with an even worse one. It didn't help that her mind was like a browser with several open tabs. There was one thing that worked for her headaches; however, she hadn't seen or heard from him in two days.

Aaron.

It didn't take long after her argument with him that day before she realized that she was in the wrong. She was always in the wrong. All Aaron was trying to do was look out for her. That was all he ever did. Her anger and frustration should not have been toward him. It should have been toward Luka.

Perhaps this was his plan. This was what he wanted. To make things worse, he was starting to cause a rift between her and her children. Jeannie didn't want to imagine what Emily would do if she found out she and Aaron had fought. That was their major concern. In fact, thinking about it, every one of them had one thing in mind.

Her happiness.

But she was the one spoiling everything with her own hands, all because she didn't know how to say no. She had lived like that for years, and it took twenty-four years of marriage for her to finally say no to Luka for the first time. It had been difficult and messy, but she did it. Now it was happening all over again.

It made Jeannie wonder if she had any self-worth at all. What did people see in her? What did Aaron see in her that she didn't see in herself? Jeannie was tired of settling, but her heart and her brain were never on the same page. How was she going to convince the people she loved—the people who had watched her go back to Luka times without number—that she wasn't even remotely thinking of being romantically involved with Luka? She only wanted to support him where she could.

No one would believe it. Heck, even she didn't believe herself. Logically, the best thing to do was ask Luka to go back to New York, find a doctor, and get treated. But emotionally, she knew that if he died after she sent him away, she'd never live it down. She'd blame herself, and it would be hard to get out of that kind of slump.

Chickadee Cove was supposed to be a clean slate.

"Jeannie! Where are you?" Jeannie heard Cathy yell from downstairs. "Come to the living room."

Lazily, Jeannie got out of the bathtub and wrapped a robe around her body. She hadn't stepped foot outside her house for two days. She had sat by her phone waiting for Aaron to call because she didn't have the nerve to call herself. But he never did, and she wouldn't accept calls from anyone else.

"What in the world, Jeannie?" Cathy said, throwing her hands in the air. "I thought you tripped, hit your head, and died or something. Why is it so hard to get ahold of you?"

Jeannie had been alone for so long, she had not realized that all her emotions had been pent up inside. Seeing Cathy released them. She scurried into her arms and cried into Cathy's shoulder.

"Oh my goodness, have you been crying?"

"I'm so stupid, Cathy. What have I done to myself?" Jeannie whispered. "I don't know what to do about this. Tell me what to do."

Cathy sat Jeannie down and dried her tears. She stayed silent for a few seconds and allowed Jeannie to gather herself.

"What's wrong? What happened?" Cathy asked. "I have been calling you to apologize for not showing up that day, but you haven't been answering me. Did something go wrong during the date?"

Jeannie shook her head. "It's not that. Aaron and I had an argument and it has been on my mind for days now. It wasn't even supposed to be that serious, but he walked out on me."

"What happened? Tell me from the start. Why did Aaron get upset?"

"Luka has cancer, Cathy."

Cathy gasped dramatically. "Cancer? Oh my goodness. That's serious."

"He says he doesn't have much time to live and he's scared."

Cathy lifted her eyebrows. "What? Luka? Scared?"

"Cathy, he genuinely looked terrified. I saw it in his eyes."

"What does he want, Jeannie?" Cathy asked. "I'm sure he didn't just come here to tell you that he was scared."

"On the night of the date with Aaron, he came to me again. He said he wanted to make amends. He wanted us to be a family again and this time, he had nothing to lose. He knew he was shameless, but he was also desperate."

Cathy groaned loudly and rose to her feet. "Jeannie, no. Come on."

"No, I didn't—It's not that," Jeannie stammered. "I didn't say yes."

"Jeannie, that saying, 'the devil you know is better than the angel you don't,' does not apply in this case. Another devil that you don't know is even better than this one that you wasted decades with."

"Listen, Cathy," she said. "I didn't say yes. In fact, I told him he was insane. What in the world do you all take me for? I might have problems of my own, but I'm not that gullible. I told him no."

"Okay," Cathy said, taking her seat. "So, what happened? Why did you and Aaron fight?"

"He found out," Jeannie said, staring at her fingers.

"Found out what?"

"That I told Luka we could be friends."

Cathy stared at Jeannie in utter disbelief. "No. You didn't actually tell him that, did you?"

"Cathy, if no one understands me, shouldn't you?"

"Understand what? Make me understand."

"I don't want to be with Luka, but I can't chase a dying man away because of our past. I don't want revenge, I just want a clean conscience. That's why I told Luka that I can only be a form of support to him."

Cathy scoffed and rose to her feet. "So, the fact that he's dying gives him permission to come back into your life?"

"Shouldn't it?" Jeannie asked, staring at her curiously.

"My dear friend." Cathy shook her head. "Did Luka need you when money was his only friend? Did he take you to Vegas when he was having the time of his life? Did you have access to him, or his money, when you needed it the most?"

"I'm not Luka. That's the thing. I can't think like him. I don't want to. We're two very different people, and while he might be the worst person, I know I'm not him."

"How do you think Aaron feels, knowing that you want to care for your sick ex-husband?"

Jeannie opened her mouth to speak but stopped. "No one understands where I'm coming from," she sobbed. "If I turn him away, it will haunt me for the rest of my life."

"Then let it haunt you. Right now, Luka is here. He may or he may not die. If he dies, you move on right. You start afresh. If he doesn't die, you're stuck with him for another couple of years till you summon the courage to leave him again. Either way, you're losing Aaron. Are you fine with that?"

"Of course, I'm not fine with it. I don't want to lose Aaron."

"Then cut Luka off, for heaven's sake, Jeannie. You can't eat your cake and eat it, too. You can't be friends with your ex-husband, who wants to get back together with you, and still be in a relationship with Aaron. You should be grateful for a man like Aaron who sees your worth more than you do. He's one of the reasons you're about to open your bakery. Can't you be selfish for once? Can you not do that? For years you have considered Luka. Stop. He's not a child. He has cancer, that sucks, but it's his cross to bear, not yours. Have you forgotten what Luka did to Lily? Have you forgotten the abuse you had to endure because of him? Maybe you should be like Luka for once and think about yourself. I am disappointed in you, Jeannie. You had a chance to tell him off for the first time since the divorce and you became friends with him. Now you've lost Aaron because of it."

Jeannie covered her face with her palm. "What do I do, Cathy?"

"Talk to Aaron. Because I will not stand by and watch you lose him. Come to an understanding with him, assure him, do whatever. But don't hurt his feelings because of someone who doesn't deserve it."

Jeannie inhaled deeply and nodded. "I'll go get dressed."

"Good. And put on some makeup, too."

<hr>

"I'm going to make amends."

Jeannie wondered if Aaron was tired of hearing her apologize. She always did something to him, and not once did he ever do anything to her that he needed to apologize for... apart from faking his identity, of course. Still, she owed him a lot, and the last thing she wanted was to get on his bad side. Aaron had easily become her favorite person aside from her children. What she felt for him was strong, and he needed to know, no matter how angry he was.

Jeannie pressed the button again and waited to hear the beep. But it was silent. She stood with her arms akimbo, staring into Aaron's home. One of his cars was missing, which meant that he was either at the sawmill or he had a business meeting somewhere else. Her best bet was to go to the sawmill and look for him there.

After standing at the bus station for nearly five minutes, Jeannie got a cab and made her way to the sawmill. She was about to text Cathy to inform her that Aaron wasn't at home when a call from Lily came in. Without hesitation, she accepted it.

"Lily!" Jeannie sighed. "You will be the death of me. What is wrong with you, young lady? Did you not think to call?"

"I'm sorry," she said. "I spoke to Dad a couple of days ago and he said he was going to talk to you. I thought he told you I'm fine."

"Did you not think to call and tell me yourself? Do you really think I want to hear about your well-being from Luka?"

"He said you both were on good terms now, so I thought he'd speak to you," Lily said. "I'm sorry. I've been super busy on set. I talked to one of the producers and he said he was going to cast me in another movie that he's currently working on. This might be it for me, Mom. My big break."

Jeannie sat back in her chair. As much as she really wanted to scold Lily, the girl was in a good mood, and she didn't want to ruin it.

"This producer...is he a good person?" Jeannie asked. "I've heard about all the dirty business that goes on in the movie industry. I don't want you getting caught up in all of that, Lily. Why not just stick to the modeling?"

"It's all a process, Mom. If I get a bit famous, and my face is on theater screens, modeling agencies won't hesitate to sign me. And don't worry about the producer. He's a good person. Dad introduced me to him before he left New York."

"Your father?" Jeannie asked. "I know the kind of company your father used to keep in New York, Lily. Be careful. Call if there's anything that you think is wrong. If it's hard and you don't think you want to do it anymore, come home. No one is forcing you."

"I know," Lily whined. "How's Dad?"

"You should know better," Jeannie said. "You talk to him all the time, don't you?"

"Mom, don't tell me you're still being stubborn about this. Dad actually said you were a feisty one, but he assured me that we'll be a family again. I know you both had your differences, but if you give him one chance—"

"Lily, I have someone else in my life," Jeannie said. She curled her fingers into a fist, hoping that Lily would take this well. "His name is Aaron, and he has been a big help to me ever since I got to Chickadee Cove. Your father has no place in my life. Right now, the only offer open to him is to be friends. Nothing more. I'm not one to hold grudges, and perhaps that's why I can still face him, but if it was someone else who went through what I went through, they might have stabbed your father in his sleep. That's how much they'd hate him. So please, don't try to play Cupid. I'd rather be alone than be with Luka. Alright?"

"Mom, how can you say that?"

"I'm not stopping you from seeing him. He's your father, do whatever you want. But you should also consider the fact that there has to be a reason your siblings and I don't want him around. You're being selfish. If you want a relationship with your father, go ahead. But leave me out of it. Just know that whatever you need, I'm here to help you because I love you. I only care about you and your siblings. You are the only ones that matter to me."

Lily took her time to respond. "Fine. I won't bring it up again."

"Thank you."

"I have to go, Mom. I'll call you later, alright?"

"Promise?"

Lily giggled. "I promise. Love you."

"Love you, too."

Jeannie hung up the call and exhaled in relief.

When she arrived at the sawmill, Jeannie paid and thanked the driver before exiting the vehicle. She made her way into the building, noticing that there was nothing going on outside. The security wasn't there, either, and most of the lights were turned off.

"Hello?" Jeannie said, stepping into the reception area. "Aaron? Is anyone here?"

"Yes?"

Jeannie gasped and swiftly turned around. Her gaze fell on a short man with a pencil behind his ear and a ruler in his hand.

"Hello," she greeted. "I'm here to see Aaron Horn."

"Mr. Horn?"

Jeannie nodded.

"He isn't here," the man revealed. "He's at the hospital."

Jeannie felt her blood chill. "What? What happened?"

"He collapsed yesterday on the field. We rushed him to the hospital and he's been there since. If you'd like, I can take a message for you."

"What hospital?"

"Uh, Chickadee Cove Memorial."

Jeannie could barely see the path in front of her but she kept walking. What if Aaron collapsed because of her? Because of their argument?

It was her fault. She had upset him.

Jeannie didn't realize that they had arrived at the hospital until the cab driver snapped her out of her thoughts. The air was cold, but she couldn't feel it. She was shivering but was sweating at the same time. If Jeannie wasn't so worried and confused, tears would have been streaming down her cheeks. She couldn't stop her hands from shaking.

Somehow, it was all her fault, and it broke Jeannie's heart. If she had called him yesterday, perhaps she would have known sooner. Aaron was already under a lot of stress, and she only added to it by arguing with him when he was trying to make her see reason. Not only did she aggravate him, but she also didn't reach out after their argument. Aaron must think the worst of her.

"Ma'am? Aren't you going to get out?" the cab driver asked her, giving her a questioning look. "We've arrived. I've said that three times."

Jeannie shook her head. "Sorry. I'm sorry. How much is it?"

After paying the cab driver, Jeannie hastily got out of

the vehicle and ran into the hospital. It was almost impossible to get her shaking under control, but Jeannie had to push through it. Her heart was pounding inside her chest, and the sound was all she could here. All she needed was to see Aaron. That was the only way she was going to calm down.

Jeannie recalled the last time she felt this anxious. It wasn't during the messy divorce she had, or the stress of moving to Chickadee Cove. It was long before that, when Lily had slumped in the middle of the road and was rushed to the hospital. Jeannie had gotten the call in the middle of a class. Till this day, she couldn't recall how she'd managed to get to the hospital. Nothing felt real until she saw that Lily was alright. Nothing else had compared to that feeling. Not until this moment.

"Hello, miss," Jeannie said to the younger lady behind the counter. "Please, I need help looking for someone. His name is Aaron Horn. He was rushed here yesterday from the sawmill."

The lady smiled at her. "One moment, please." She lowered her head and typed on her computer for a couple of seconds before lifting her head back up. "What's your relationship with Mr. Horn?"

Jeannie swallowed. "I'm...he is my boyfriend. We..." she stuttered. "Sorry, I'm Jeannie Miller. I—"

For some reason, she was running out of air. Jeannie paused, took in a deep breath, and forced a smile. "Is he alright?" she managed to ask. "I heard he collapsed. Is he not taking visitors? If I could just see him for a bit to make sure he's alright."

"Please, come with me," the nurse said.

Jeannie followed her without hesitation. She didn't consider the fact that Aaron might not want to see her. Their last conversation didn't end well, and Aaron practically stormed out of her house without answering her question.

Perhaps Aaron didn't want to see Jeannie half as much as she was dying to see him.

It didn't matter, however. Jeannie had made up her mind not to leave Aaron's side even if he asked her to. She was going to apologize to him, beg him if she must. Part of the reason she felt completely devastated by the incident was that she couldn't think of one thing she had done for Aaron. He was always the one going out of his way for her; with the bakery, keeping her company, taking her on dates, making her feel special. All she had managed to do was put him in a hospital. It wasn't fair. Aaron deserved better. *She* had to do better.

They walked down a long hallway, and Jeannie followed the nurse closely. She tripped on air when she noticed a familiar figure walking by at the end of the hall. Jeannie squinted to see better and caught a glimpse of the person's face before she disappeared around the corner.

"Isabel?" she mumbled.

What is she doing here?

Jeannie shook her head vigorously. She had more pressing matters to worry about, and Isabel's business was not her concern.

The nurse pushed the trolley to a private room and stood at the side of the door. She gestured for Jeannie to go in, and Jeannie thanked her before stepping into the room.

"Jeannie?"

Hearing Aaron's voice felt like a cold bath on an extremely hot day. Relief washed over Jeannie's body. She stood still and stared at Aaron wired up to machines. He had a confused look on his face, but Jeannie could see his eye bags, his chapped lips, and she could hear the crack in his voice.

"Oh no, Aaron," Jeannie cried, rushing over to his side. She scanned him from head to toe, feeling a pang in her heart. "Why are you in a hospital gown? Why do you look so weak? What are all these machines? Are you dying?"

Aaron's confused frown suddenly turned into a smile and he snorted. "Am I dying?"

At that point, Jeannie couldn't hold back the tears anymore. "I—I heard you fainted at the sawmill. Did you hit your head? What happened?" She sobbed.

The smile on Aaron's face faded when he saw Jeannie in tears. "No, Jeannie, I'm fine. I'm completely fine. Well...not completely, but I'm getting better. I just have a really stubborn and weak heart."

"What?" Jeannie sniffed. "Is there a problem with your heart?"

"It's my high blood pressure," Aaron stuttered and lowered his head. "I technically haven't been religious with my pills."

Jeannie smacked Aaron on the hand. "Why not? Aaron, the last thing you should be playing with is your medication. You don't watch what you eat, you only eat pizza...wine, and on top of all that, you're not taking your medicine? Are you trying to kill yourself?"

"But I'm in great shape, aren't I?" he teased.

"Does it matter? You're still in the hospital, and you had me very worried. I thought something horrible happened. I thought when you slumped, you hit your head, and you cracked it open."

Aaron placed his hand over hers. "I'm sorry for worrying you. I forgot to take my pills and I've been so busy at work. I promise, I'll do better this time."

Jeannie stared at the ground. "I figured it was my fault. I worried I'd made you upset when you couldn't handle it. I apologize, Aaron. I—I wasn't thinking. I was just talking, and I didn't take your feelings into consideration. I'm sorry."

"No, no, Jeannie. Don't think like that," Aaron answered and scanned the room. "Would you grab that chair at the corner of the room, please?"

Jeannie obliged. She walked over to the corner, got the chair, brought it to the side of the bed, and sat. "You're not angry with me?"

Aaron took her hand into his. "Of course not."

Jeannie gave him a knowing look. "That's a lie."

"No, it's not."

"Yes, it is. You have a tell."

Perhaps it was the years of studying her children that made it easy to tell when someone was lying. Aaron made it obvious. He would bite his lower lip when he was unsure of something before he said it. Jeannie had noticed it only twice, mainly because Aaron was always honest with her. But she could tell when he was withholding information.

Aaron tilted his head to the side. "A tell?"

"It doesn't matter," Jeannie said. "I'm sorry for upsetting you, Aaron."

Aaron sighed and twiddled with Jeannie's fingers. "I'm sorry, too, Jeannie. Honestly. I feel so terrible."

"You have no reason to apologize, Aaron. In hindsight, you've never actually offended me. Ever. I'm the one being so emotional."

"No, I should apologize," Aaron told her. "What I said to you right before I left was uncalled for. I was upset, you're right. But that gave me no right to say that to you. I'm sorry."

Jeannie shook her head slowly. "You had a point. Deep down, I know what you said was right. I can be a pushover. I can be overly sentimental. I've been working on it for years, and I thought I had my emotions under control, but I don't. I'm starting to think that's just the way I am."

"There's nothing wrong with the way you are," Aaron said. "The only issue is that people tend to take advantage of that particular trait, and that fault isn't on you. But you have got to start creating boundaries and sticking to them, Jeannie."

Jeannie squeezed his hand. "I will."

"Promise?"

"I promise," she answered. "Are you sure you're alright? What did the doctor say? I should have called you yesterday, I'm so sorry. I should have known."

"Stop apologizing already." Aaron chuckled and coughed. "I'm fine. I'm going to be discharged soon, with a warning from the doctor to take my pills religiously. I'm okay."

Jeannie took in a deep breath and exhaled in relief. "That's good news. I'm glad it's nothing serious."

An awkward silence ensued afterward. Jeannie stared everywhere but at Aaron's face. All she had thought about on her way to the hospital was Aaron's health, and now that she had confirmed he was fine, she had no idea what to say. One thing was clear, however, and that was the fact that she felt something really strong for Aaron.

The issue was that Jeannie couldn't put it in words. She had never done that with anyone other than Luka. She was unsure of what to say. She didn't want to come on too strong, and she didn't want to chase Aaron away at the same time.

"Do you want to talk about it?" Aaron asked, finally breaking the long silence. "Do you want to talk about us...and Luka? You know, this situation?"

"I'm confused," Jeannie admitted with a sigh. "I'm confused, Aaron."

Aaron's eyebrows furrowed. "About your feelings?"

"What? No," Jeannie said. "Not that. About what's right and what's wrong. I haven't been myself lately, and I can admit that. But I'm not confused about you. I'm sure."

Aaron adjusted on the bed. "What are you sure about?"

Jeannie bit her lower lip. The last thing she wanted was to chase Aaron away, but if she didn't commit to something—to their relationship—he was going to walk away on his own.

Then she'd lose him. She couldn't lose him. He was one of the few good things in her life.

"Jeannie, you want to say something," Aaron said, staring at her. "You have a tell, too. You bite your lip when you're nervous."

"I do? Then we have the same tell," Jeannie said.

"Oh." Aaron chuckled. "I've never noticed that about myself. I'm usually never nervous. Well, I get nervous around you, but that's pretty normal. I mean—"

"I think I'm in love with you, Aaron," Jeannie revealed, interrupting him. "This—I don't recognize this feeling I have for you. It's not what I feel for my children, or Cathy. It's stronger than what I felt when I was in love decades ago. It's not...what young love felt like. Perhaps that's why I was so confused. I only remember what love felt like when I was young. But I'm getting the hang of it now. I think I'm in love with you, and I'm sorry I'm admitting to my feelings this late. It's not the most romantic setting, but...I thought you should know."

Aaron was still with his mouth ajar as he stared at her. Slowly, the corners of his lips began to tilt upward, and he displayed his perfect set of white teeth.

"Thank...you," he managed to say.

Jeannie giggled, amused by his awkward response. "Why are you thanking me?"

"Do you need me to confess my feelings, too, or..."

"No." She continued giggling as she shook her head. "I think you've made it pretty obvious many times."

"Well, I love you," Aaron said. "I really do, and I've been sure about you since the first day I saw you. It warms my heart to hear you speak this way."

Jeannie took his hand into hers and stared at it. "With that out of the way, I should tell you that if you happened to have the ring here with you, and you proposed again, I would agree to your proposal."

"Is that a yes?" Aaron asked quietly.

Jeannie glanced at him and nodded. "It is."

Her attempt to hide her visibly flushed cheeks failed when Aaron placed his hand on her chin and tilted her head toward him. He paused for a few seconds to stare into her eyes. Then he lowered his head, and Jeannie instinctively shut her eyes.

When their lips touched, her thought train immediately took a trip to the clouds. It felt like a bolt of electricity travelled through her body and woke up every cell. Jeannie parted her lips slightly to take more of Aaron in as she held on tighter than necessary to the bedsheet. Aaron caressed her cheek with his thumb, causing the hair on Jeannie's skin to stand on end. She hadn't felt like this in so long. The calming effect of his touch was surreal.

"It's too bad I don't have the ring with me right now," Aaron whispered, breaking the kiss. "But I will bring it to you as soon as I get out of this place. I promise."

It took a couple of seconds for Jeannie's head to return from the clouds. "Right. No, you can take your time," she stammered.

Aaron nodded. "I was going to watch an old movie. Would you like to join me? I know it's getting pretty late, but—"

"I'm not leaving," Jeannie blurted. "I mean, we'll leave together. Tomorrow morning."

"Are you sure? You don't mind?"

"Not at all," she answered. "Besides, you'll need someone to help, and I'll be glad to."

Aaron smiled brightly. "That's good to hear. Come on," he said, throwing the covers aside.

Jeannie glanced at the side of the bed, and then looked back at Aaron. "You want me to lie with you? Are you sure that's alright? I mean, you're technically a patient, and if the nurse walks in—"

"It's alright," he said. "Come on."

Jeannie didn't hesitate. She climbed into the bed and snuggled into Aaron's arms. It felt right, like something she didn't know she needed until she got to experience it. Dating was the last thing on Jeannie's mind when she first moved to Chickadee Cove, but now she couldn't think of anywhere else she'd rather be than here with Aaron.

Chapter Twelve

*T*wo *Days Later...*

"Have you taken your medication this morning, Aaron?" Jeannie asked, wedging the phone between her ear and shoulder as she separated the boxes of oranges from the apples. "Remember what the doctor said, right?"

"I remember," Aaron answered. "I took them this morning."

"Are you lying?"

"Yes, I actually forgot, but I'm taking then right now," he answered. "Do you want to video call me instead?"

"No," Jeannie answered. "I trust you."

"That's...nice, but I'm also asking because I want to see your face. I miss you."

Jeannie stifled a smile. "We were together all through yesterday. You even refused to work. I think you can go a day without seeing me."

"Well, I'm not so sure about that," he teased. "Remember? The last time I didn't hear from you for two days, I passed out. Do you want that to repeat itself? You don't, do you?"

Jeannie giggled and then choked on her laughter when she

spotted Cathy giving her knowing, suspicious looks. "How about tonight? I'll make you a healthy dinner, and we'll have it at your house."

"Why my house? So you can be sure that I'm taking my medication?"

"Yes, Mr. Horn," said Jeannie. "If I have to treat you like a child until you get better, then that I will do. I'll see you at seven."

"Are you stopping by the market?" Aaron asked. "I can come over and pick you up at...let's say six, and we'll go together. What do you think?"

"You have a meeting at the sawmill at six, Aaron," Jeannie told him. "Or did you forget? That client in Florida that you told me about yesterday. He set up a conference call at six to discuss the terms of the contract you drew up."

"Right," Aaron whispered. "I could—"

"No," Jeannie shut him down. "You're not shifting it because you want to go grocery shopping with me. Have your meeting. I'll make something delicious for you when you get home. I'll even let you have some white wine. But only a little. That's if you close the contract."

"Well, I've technically never gone grocery shopping with a lady before," Aaron said. "If you think about it, that's more important, isn't it? Creating that core memory for me."

Jeannie covered her face with her palm and shook her head. "How are you so successful, Aaron?"

"I'm smart," he answered.

"You think?"

"If I do say so myself."

Jeannie rolled her eyes and smirked. "Get ready for your meeting. I'll see you at seven."

"Fine." Aaron sighed. "I'll see you at seven."

"Bye."

Jeannie set the phone down on the counter. She found it

difficult to stop smiling. If she had known that love could do that for someone, perhaps she would have tried to find it sooner. Her thoughts were filled with Aaron, and she frequently caught herself reminiscing about their times together and smiling. It was silly, childish, but Jeannie didn't mind. She didn't mind at all.

"I don't know what it is, or what Aaron did to you, but it's so obvious."

Jeannie had expected Cathy to chime in. It took her long enough.

"Don't be dramatic. Aaron and I are taking things really slow."

Cathy took her seat on the stool by Jeannie's side. "Really? You're practically glowing at this point. Look at you, smiling. You've been smiling for two days straight. That's not normal."

Jeannie raised her eyebrows. "How isn't it normal? Don't you smile all the time with your husband? Doesn't he give you butterflies in your stomach like they write about in all those romance books? Isn't that why you married him?"

"It was," Cathy said. "But right now, all he does is find new, innovative ways to annoy me."

Jeannie snorted as she continued sorting the apples into a separate box. "What does that even mean?"

Cathy stuffed her hand into the box, too. "Well, it started a while back when I realized that my dearest husband wore his socks and shoes like a maniac. He puts on a sock, and then a shoe first, and then does the other leg. A normal human being does a sock and a sock, and a shoe and a shoe. It drives me crazy, but he won't stop."

Jeannie squinted her eyes. "What is so wrong about doing that, Cathy?"

"You don't get it." Cathy shook her head. "Nowadays… like I said, he has found other ways to drive me crazy. He doesn't take his clothes off in one place. I'd find his trousers in the living room, his shirt in the bedroom, a sock in the kitchen, and the other one in the laundry basket. It drives me nuts. I mean, I have to clean up after the children, but my husband doesn't make it any easier."

Jeannie chuckled. "Well, there have got to be things that he does that make you smile."

Cathy paused to think. "Probably the little things. He never comes back home emptyhanded. He gets my favorite tacos, or wine, or something. That makes me smile. So, it's not all bad."

"See?" Jeannie said.

"Soon, Aaron is going to start annoying you, too. It's just a matter of time and living together."

Jeannie shook her head. "I doubt that. Aaron is...near perfect. I like everything he does."

"So did I," Cathy said. "You'll see. I don't have to tell you all about my married life."

Jeannie sighed. If only she had experienced all that Cathy was whining about in her first marriage; perhaps it wouldn't sound that foreign to her now. Jeannie didn't know what it was like to have petty arguments with her husband. All the times she argued with Luka were about serious issues, nothing playful at all. The things he did that annoyed her were grounds for divorce, not the things Cathy was explaining that only got on her nerves.

"I know what you're thinking," Cathy said without looking up. "You're thinking that it's probably too late to start experiencing all these things I'm talking about. You're regretting your life choices. I understand that, but I'd like to clarify something. It's not too late. I promise you. Good things happen to good people, that's why you have Aaron now. If you think about it, you both are perfect for each other. He didn't get to experience what a real family felt like, and you didn't get to experience what a loving husband felt like. It's new for the both of you. Enjoy it. How many times do I have to tell you that you deserve it, Jeannie?"

"I'm not wallowing in self-pity, Cathy. I'm past that," Jeannie told her. "Right now, I'm looking forward to the future."

"A future without Luka, right?"

Jeannie groaned. "Let's not talk about Luka right now, Cathy. Please?"

"You know people are talking, right?" Cathy asked.

"I don't care."

"Yes, you do."

"Maybe I do," Jeannie admitted. "Maybe I don't. Let's not talk about Luka right now. We have a bakery opening to plan. The donut cutters, baguettes, and Bundt pans just arrived, and we have a lot of fruits to sort out and store. We have to juice some, too. We have a lot to do before the opening, and I don't want my mood all over the place. I need to focus."

"How do you expect to do that when your ex-husband is strolling in and out of your house? It's not a good look, Jeannie. I'm not doing this to ruin your mood, but you know that sooner or later, you will have to make a decision or it will make itself. That's how things work. If you leave unfinished business for so long, they eventually sort themselves out. You don't want that. Take a hold of things, for Christ's sake. Like I said, it's not a good look. You're in a relationship now. How do you think Aaron feels?"

"I'm not doing anything," Jeannie said, frustrated.

"That's the point. You're not doing anything. Didn't you hear all I just said about unfinished business? Do something about him. Tell him off, send him away. Tell him to stop coming to your house, offer moral support from across the country. Luka can't be around you."

"Luka, Luka, Luka..." Jeannie took in a deep breath.

"Cathy, please. I'm sick and tired of hearing about this man. Can we please drop it?"

"Speak of the devil," Cathy rasped, rising to her feet.

Jeannie turned around in time to catch Luka walking into her shop. He had a smug look on his face, as always, with his hands behind him. Luka walked up to them and smiled.

"Good morning, beautiful ladies," he greeted and turned to Cathy. "Cathy, long time, no see."

Cathy turned to Jeannie, completely ignoring Luka. "You can't ignore it," she said. "This one will not go away."

With that, Cathy got up and walked away, not uttering another word. Aaron chuckled and shook his head as he sat in her place.

"She never really liked me, that one," he mumbled.

"Why do you think?" Jeannie asked, pushing the box of apples aside. "Why are you here, Luka?"

Luka's smile waned. "It breaks my heart every single time when you look at me like this, Jeannie. Like I'm dirty. I'm human. I make mistakes, but I don't think I deserve this hostility from the only woman that I love."

Jeannie mellowed. "Why are you here, Luka?"

"Let me help," Luka offered. "I'm good with everything. I can paint, fix things..."

"There's nothing to paint, and there's nothing that needs fixing. As you can see, everything is already in order. I don't need any help."

"Oh, come on, my love. There has to be something that you need help with. You need money? I can give you some."

Jeannie turned to face him. "Actually, Luka, I've been thinking. You have money, you can buy all the care you need. Shouldn't you be in a hospital?"

Luka nodded slowly. His countenance changed, and it seemed as if he had lost all his confidence.

"That's actually why I came here," he revealed. "I need

to go to New York for my prognosis. It's Hillview Hospital in Soho, I, uh...I've been putting it off for the longest time because, as much as I hate to admit it, I'm terrified. I mean, I know I'm sick, and my chances of surviving are slim, but I don't want to hear it. I know, it's stupid."

Seeing him like that, so vulnerable, with fear evident in his eyes, made Jeannie feel bad for him. The thought of death would scare anyone. Luka was human after all.

"I'm so sorry, Luka," Jeannie said. "But you need to see a doctor, no matter how terrified you are. The sooner you get treated, the better."

"I know," he answered. "I came here to ask you to accompany me, Jeannie. I don't want to hear it alone. I know it's selfish of me to ask you this, but you're the only support that I have. Please, it will only be for a week. No funny business. I need you."

"I understand that you're scared, Luka. But I can't go with you," Jeannie said. "The bakery is set to open in a week, I have people to interview, recipes to start practicing, stuff to buy. I can't leave Chickadee Cove. No offense, but you really think I'd leave all of this behind to go with you to New York? I'll support you however I can, but I can't go with you. I'm sorry."

Luka shrugged his shoulders. "It was worth a shot. Can I ask that you call me instead? I just need to hear your voice. You have no idea what it does for me. Please."

Jeannie paused, then slowly nodded. "I can do that," she said. "I'll call you to follow up."

"Promise?"

"Sure," she responded. "Go home and rest. You need it, and I have work to do. I have to finish sorting and storing these fruits by the end of today, so they don't go bad."

"I can help," Luka offered, inching closer. "Let me."

"No," Jeannie said, rising to her feet. "Cathy is in the back waiting for me. We'll do it together. Go home, Luka."

Luka rose to his feet, too. "You know you've never asked me where I'm staying. Aren't you curious?"

Jeannie shrugged her shoulders. "No. I'm sure you're taking very good care of yourself."

"I miss when you used to do that. You know, take good care of me. Do you remember?"

Jeannie felt the hair on her skin rise. "Luka, when I think of our past, it's not happy memories that come to mind. So, I'd advise that you don't ask me to recall anything. It's never pleasant."

Before Jeannie could react, Luka reached for her hand and took it. "How can I make it up to you? Jeannie, I'm serious about us. About our family. Do you think I'm comfortable with my children hating me? Emily, Mason, and Kelly don't talk to me. Kelly didn't even invite me to her wedding. Shouldn't we have a second chance to make it work before I..." Luka swallowed.

Subtly, Jeannie slipped her hand away from Luka's grasp and took a step back. Luka was starting to get to her. She hadn't realized that he had made so much progress until that very moment—when he touched her hand, and she didn't immediately pull away in disgust.

"Everyone deserves a second chance, Jeannie," he said.

Jeannie scoffed. "A second chance? *Second*?"

"You know what I mean," he said. "I'll see you when I get back. Hopefully, with good news. If you need anything, anything at all, please don't hesitate to reach out to me. I love you, Jeannie. I'm being sincere this time about my intentions. I hope you see it."

With that, Luka exited the bakery and got into his car. Jeannie watched him drive off before crashing back down on her chair. She could hear footsteps approaching, then they stopped abruptly.

Jeanne turned to the side to find Cathy with her arms crossed and her head tilted to the side judgmentally.

"Don't look at me like that," Jeannie said, fiddling with her fingers. "I know already."

Chapter Thirteen

A Week Later...

"Yes, the opening is today. I'm so excited, but I really would have wanted you to be here, Lily."

Jeannie stared at her ring as she conversed with Lily on the phone. Aaron had put it on her finger exactly a week ago, and she had formed a routine of admiring the precious stone every morning, at noon, and right before she went to bed. If she ever needed a reason to smile, she'd look at it, and then a thought of Aaron would come to mind. Jeannie feared she was getting too attached to the ring, but she was fine with it.

"I'm sorry, Mom," Lily apologized. "But I know it'll be great. How does the place look?"

Jeannie scanned the bakery and brought a hand to her hip. "Well, we had to move most of the chairs and the tables to create a floor space. Cathy and I spent all night tying up red, blue, and white balloons, and everywhere is covered with them. There's a ribbon in front, which I'll cut soon. I wanted a chandelier, but Cathy thought it was over the top and a lot of stress, so we just settled for orange and white lightbulbs, to add color. Everything is set. I baked a lot of pastries, and I spent all morning going around with Aaron giving out samples to my neighbors. Now we're set for the opening."

"What are you wearing?"

"Jeannie looked down at her gown. "I'm wearing a blue pleated gown. Why do you ask?"

"No reason," Lily answered. "I was just wondering. Have fun tonight, Mom. I wish I was there with you. I wish we were all there with you as a family."

"Thank you, honey."

Lily had started to call more often. It surprised Jeannie, but she was glad, even if it meant listening to Lily go on and on about what a changed man Luka was, and how he was the perfect dad. She was still attempting to play Cupid, but Jeannie had a way of ignoring Lily's hints. All she wanted was to talk to her daughter and be sure she was alright.

"Have you talked to Emily, Mason, and Kelly?"

Jeannie sighed. "Well, I've talked to Mason and Kelly, and they congratulated me. Emily still hasn't called."

The best Jeannie had received from her first child were text messages for the past two weeks. Emily was angry, and it was the first time she had gone that long without speaking to Jeannie. It was obvious why she was upset, and Jeannie couldn't fault her for it, but it broke her heart.

"Which reminds me," Jeannie said. "Lily, when last did you talk to your siblings? You never answer when we set up a group call. Do you even speak to them?"

"Of course, I do," Lily answered.

"Lily..." Jeannie called her out.

"Alright fine," Lily groaned. "But it's not my fault. We used to talk once in a while, but lately, they refuse to take my calls or speak to me."

"And why is that?" Jeannie asked.

"How should I know?"

"When you call them, Lily, do you do the same thing you

always do when you speak to me? Try to cajole them to hear your father out?"

Lily took her time to answer. "I'm not forcing them to do anything, but it's pretty heartless of them to ignore him like he's nobody. No matter what he did, he's still their father, and they are being big babies. I mean, isn't it time they grew up and put the past behind them?"

Jeannie massaged her forehead. If only Lily knew that it was because of her...because of what Luka did to her...

"Mom? Are you listening?" Lily asked.

"I am, honey," Jeannie said. "Please, don't ruin your relationship with your siblings because of this stunt you're trying to pull. If they don't want to, then they don't want to. Leave Luka out of this, and just talk to them like you used to."

"You know it's because of you they are acting like this, Mom? If you would just talk to them—"

"Lily," Jeannie interrupted her. "It's my bakery's opening. It's a happy, unproblematic day. I'd like to keep it that way. I'll send you pictures and videos after the event. Love you."

"Love you, Mom. Congratulations once again."

Jeannie hung up the phone and shut her eyes. She had vowed not to let anything ruin her evening. The bakery opening was one event she'd looked forward to ever since she arrived in Chickadee Cove. It was her lifelong dream come true. A special day, with a personal, special reason.

Just then, Jeannie's phone rang. "Oh, thank goodness," she breathed.

"Hi, Mom."

"Emily Miller. Is this your way of torturing me?" Jeannie asked. "You refused to call me or answer my calls for two weeks. Is this how you treat your mother?"

"I sent you text messages, Mom."

"That's not the point. The point is, you are still upset with me and that breaks my heart."

"Mom, congratulations on your bakery opening," Emily said, changing the subject. "We all know you deserve this, and I'm glad to see your dream come to reality. It's a good thing that you prioritized your peace of mind and your happiness over everything. I hope you will be able to do that in all areas of your life and be completely happy."

"Thank you," Jeannie responded quietly. "I see what you did with your last sentence. Emily, I know this is about your father, but—"

"My father?" Emily scoffed. "Is that what you now refer to him as? When have I ever called him that?"

"I'm sorry," Jeannie apologized. "I was on a call with Lily a few seconds ago, and...I'm sorry. Let's not fight anymore, alright? Let me handle this myself. I am not a child, Emily. I can figure this out. I don't want to fight with you. It's a happy day."

"It is a happy day," Emily said. "Which is why I don't want to talk about this. It's your day. Besides, I'm not listening to anything so long as Luka is still in Chickadee Cove by your side. It will never make sense to me."

"Emily, he is sick. Explain to me how I'm supposed to say 'leave my life forever, Luka, I don't care that you're dying of cancer' to a sick man? It's cruel."

"Enjoy your day, Mom. Try not to think too much," Emily said and ended the call.

"Wait, Emily—"

Jeannie clenched her jaw. "She has such a temper."

"Who does?"

Jeannie gasped, startled by the voice just behind her. Her shock turned to delight when she saw Aaron dressed in a nice midnight black tuxedo. He looked so breathtaking in his fitted suit and with his slicked-back hair that Jeannie felt like swooning in his arms.

"Goodness gracious," she managed to say. "Who is opening a bakery again? I'm confused."

"I believe it to be my woman, Miss Miller," Aaron answered. "I'm really proud of her, and I cannot wait for her to start living her dream."

Jeannie wrapped her arms around his waist and hugged him tightly. There was still that feeling she got when she was around him. The peace and quiet that came with being in his arms. It was a feeling she could never get enough of.

"The place looks beautiful, Jeannie," Aaron noted. "Congratulations. I brought you a basket of flowers. They are on the table by the kitchen. I thought I'd find you there."

"Thank you," Jeannie said, snuggling into his chest. "I was on a call with Lily, and with Emily."

"They called to congratulate you?"

Jeannie nodded. "Why don't I feel as excited as I thought I would be? I mean, I imagined this happening countless times, and I was looking forward to it. I'm happy, but I'm not jumping around like I thought I'd be."

Aaron stroked her hair. "The fact that you're not feeling what you imagined doesn't mean you're not happy at all. Life is just different from the way we imagine things. Don't worry. This right here is just the start. It gets better and you'll get happier."

"Thank you," Jeannie said again. She pulled away from his embrace and met his gaze. "What about your guests? You said you were inviting a few people."

"They'll be here once it starts," he replied. "But make that a couple. Not a few."

Jeannie arched her eyebrows. "A couple? What did you do, Aaron?"

Aaron stuffed his hands into his pocket and stepped back. "Well, for one, I ordered a bunch of flowers. They should be here soon to decorate the place with them. I bought a lot of white roses, actually. Then I invited some of my friends over. They are down-to-Earth people, you know, friendly and whatnot."

"Aaron, I've met people you call friends. Sure, they are down-to-Earth, but so are their pockets. They are not middle class citizens like me, are they?"

Aaron stammered. "Well...no. They are pretty...I invited Fortune Marshall and his wife. Then about three other people...and their partners. Then lastly, Sofia Matthews."

Jeannie's jaw dropped to the floor. "Fortune Marshall?"

"You were the one who asked me to invite my friends because you didn't know a lot of people here."

"Fortune Marshall?" Jeannie repeated. "The Fortune Marshall of Maine? Probably the wealthiest man in Maine? Business mogul? *That* Fortune Marshall?"

Aaron scratched the back of his head. "Okay, I'll admit that I did that to impress you."

"Sofia Matthews is a news anchor. You invited a celebrity?" Jeannie asked.

Aaron squinted his eyes. "I can't tell if you're angry, indifferent, or excited."

"Of course, I'm excited. These people are going to taste my pastries and cakes. You know how exciting that is? My heart is pounding, Aaron."

Aaron smiled proudly. "I'm glad you're fine with it. Plus, I've tasted your pastries and they are out of this world. You're good at what you do, Jeannie. I'm excited to see your progress for this next chapter of your life."

"You know I couldn't have done all of this without you, right?" Jeannie said with a smile. "Thank you for giving me a chance, too. I don't know how things would have turned out if you hadn't agreed to my request the first day we met."

"I'm glad I did," Aaron said. "I'm glad I was there that day and not Frank."

"I'm glad, too."

Aaron stroked Jeannie's back. "You got this. The bakery looks really beautiful."

Jeannie scanned the place. "I can't wait to cut that ribbon," she squeaked. "I've made friends with all of the neighbors. I gave them samples this morning, and I got some feedback. They love them. Hopefully, I'll turn all of them into loyal customers."

"You will." He nodded.

An hour later, the bakery was filled with people. Aaron said he invited a couple of people, but those people came with other people, other important people that Jeannie actually recognized from the television. When the crowd was ready, they exited the bakery to officially cut the ribbon and open the shop. Jeannie received a ton of applause, and she had to fight to hold back her tears. Two years ago, she would have scoffed at the thought of ever achieving this dream. She had never thought she'd summon the courage to chase her dream, given her age and all the limitations. But she was able to take that step by cutting off all her baggage.

Well, some of her baggage.

"Jeannie, please come," Aaron called for her. He was standing with a group of people in the middle of the room while she went around greeting her guests.

Jeannie walked over to Aaron's side, and he took her hand.

"Jeannie, I'd like to introduce you to Dr. Fortune Marshall of Steed Pharmaceuticals, Mr. Edwin Sharma, he's a surgeon at Hope hospital, and Sofia Matthews. You should recognize her from NBS news."

Jeannie swallowed. They were all staring at her. Jeannie had not realized how socially awkward she could get until that very moment when she needed to say something and her mind was completely blank.

"It's really an honor to meet all of you," she finally said.

"I'm truly grateful that you could take the time to come to my bakery opening."

Aaron turned to them. "This is Jeannie Miller, the owner of the bakery and my girlfriend."

"I just had some of your apple pie," Sofia said. "You are good, Miss Miller."

Jeannie felt a tingle in her stomach. "Oh, please. Call me Jeannie. And thank you for the compliment. Trust me, it means so much to me. I hope you visit sometime soon."

Aaron placed his hand on the small of Jeannie's back and pulled her closer to him. "I invited these particular people because they are obsessed with pastries. Easy customers, Jeannie."

Fortune chuckled and shook his head. "Well, Aaron's not wrong. I might not be able to visit every day, but I will stop by every time I can. You made delicious food, and I'm impressed."

"Ah, Fortune is usually not an easy man to impress," Edwin chimed in. "But I tasted the apple pie, too, so I understand where they are both coming from. You're going to be seeing more of me, Miss Miller."

Jeannie had so much she wanted to say in response to their kind words, but she was too focused on Aaron's hand on her back. There was a feeling that came with it, one she had craved for so long. It felt as if Aaron had just declared her to the entire world as his woman. He was proud to be seen with her. Jeannie had been deprived of that for so long that it almost drove her to the verge of tears. She wasn't destined to be alone after all.

"Excuse us," Aaron said. He pulled Jeannie to the side and placed both hands on her shoulders. "Are you alright, Jeannie? You seem a bit...distracted."

Jeannie felt tears sting her eyes. "Thank you," she whispered.

Aaron sighed in relief. "I thought something was wrong. You don't have to keep thanking me for every little thing, Jeannie. I didn't force them to like your food, you did that on your own."

"That's not why I'm thanking you," she clarified and inhaled deeply. "I'm just overwhelmed with a lot of emotions today. I'm happy, I'm sad…I feel loved, I'm worried, I'm relieved. But the good thing is that my happiness overshadows everything else."

"That's all that matters," Aaron told her. "With time, you'll sort out everything else. But right now, focus on this right here. By the way, where in the world is Cathy? She was more excited for the opening than anyone else."

Jeannie sighed. "Her son's sick. She had to take him to the doctor. I'm sure it's nothing serious, but she promised to be here with him soon. She'll come."

"Alright. Now, I don't know what you're thinking about, but I want you to stop. Live in this moment and just…be. You have a bakery now. Like you've always wanted."

Jeannie sighed and leaned on Aaron's chest. Opening the bakery was only the start. Running the bakery was the real work. Jeannie was excited about the times that were going to come, but there was still that uneasy feeling in the pit of her stomach that she couldn't quite get rid of.

Chapter Fourteen

"You say she's angry with you?"

It was a Sunday. Jeannie and Aaron had just concluded the final rounds of interviews for prospective employees at the bakery, and they had hired six people in total: two bakers, two salespersons, a delivery boy, and a receptionist. They were to come back the next day to learn about their various assignments. Jeannie felt relieved, knowing that that chapter was closed and everything was finally set. She had checked off all the boxes on her list, and it was time to actually run the bakery.

"Yes," Jeannie said, nodding. "Emily rarely gets angry with me, but she's upset, and it's my fault."

They sat by the window of the bakery eating a pot pie that Jeannie had made earlier that day. Aaron had arrived as soon as Jeannie opened the shop, and he was the one who asked the questions they used to judge the employees. Jeannie figured that it was only ideal that she reward him for all his hard work.

"What did you do to get her angry?" Aaron asked, setting his spoon down. "If, like you said, Emily rarely gets mad, then you must have done something to make her upset. What did you do? Figure that out first, and then you can try to fix it. Tell me what you did."

Jeannie was starting to regret telling Aaron about her squabble with Emily. It was about Luka, and she was trying very hard not to bring up her ex-husband around her current partner. Luka was the cause of their most recent fight, and Jeannie feared that talking about him was going to start another one.

"It's about Luka, isn't it?" Aaron asked, keeping his gaze on the pot pie. "Emily is angry that you refuse to cut him off?"

Jeannie gasped. "Did Mason tell you?"

Aaron lifted his eyes and nodded. "He did. I didn't want to mention it until you were comfortable talking about it. You weren't planning to tell me, were you?"

"I was going to tell you," Jeannie countered. "I'm the one who brought it up, wasn't I? She's angry that Luka is still around."

Aaron raised his eyebrows. "Jeannie...Is Emily angry that Luka is still around, or is she angry that you are talking to him?"

Jeannie scratched her nape. "A little bit of both," she mumbled. "But I have it under control."

Aaron squinted his eyes. "What does that even mean?"

"It means you shouldn't worry about it," Jeannie said, reaching for his hand. "Luka isn't a threat to you, or a threat to us. He's just my annoying ex-husband who happens to be sick. Don't let it bother you. Honestly, I don't like talking about Luka with you. He is my past. That's all there is to it."

Aaron adjusted in his seat and bit his lower lip. "I'm going to say it. I'm not comfortable with him around you, Jeannie. It might just be my jealousy, it might be something else, but I won't lie to you. I don't mean to offend you by saying this but, given how many times Luka found a way back into your life in the past, it makes me uneasy that he has this much access to you right now."

"What do you mean, access?" Jeannie asked with a stern tone.

"Don't get defensive," Aaron said softly. "You tend to get defensive when we talk about him, which is another reason I'm uncomfortable."

Jeannie mellowed and sat back into her chair. "I'm sorry. I wasn't getting defensive. I just...I really don't like talking about Luka, Aaron. Let's dwell on something else. Like you. What are you up to? How do you have so much free time? I know you, Aaron. I know how busy you can be. But I've been seeing so much of you, it's starting to scare me. If I didn't know any better, my guess would be that you got fired. But you can't get fired, so what's up?"

Aaron leaned on his chair and smiled. "I just have a lot of free time, and I choose to spend it with you, my girlfriend. Is that a problem?"

Jeannie drew circles on the table with her fingers. "Not that I'm complaining or anything, but it seems as if I'm hindering you from actually working, and that is the last thing I ever want to do. You know you don't have to come by all the time, right? We can meet up whenever it's convenient for you."

Aaron shrugged his shoulders. "It's convenient for me now."

Jeannie tilted her head to the side. "Really? You're saying you have nothing to do right now?"

"Nothing else I'd rather be doing," he answered.

His statement caused her cheeks to flush crimson. Jeannie looked away, avoiding his gaze. "I'm starting to think that you're a flirt, Aaron Horn."

Aaron gasped dramatically and placed a hand on his chest. "Me? A flirt? What have I done to deserve such an accusation?

My only crime is falling for your charms. If anything, *you're* the flirt. You seduced me, and now I can't think of or do anything else. You're the real criminal here, Jeannie Miller."

Jeannie threw her head back laughing. "Okay, you took it way too far. I was only joking. What I meant to say is that you're really smooth with your words, and I'm embarrassed because I'm obviously affected by them. You're the charmer, not me."

Aaron nodded. "I'll take that. I am pretty charming."

"Yes indeed." Jeannie giggled.

Aaron took her hand and caressed it. "So, how's Cathy? She didn't make it to the opening after all. Is her child alright? Anything serious?"

Jeannie glanced at her phone. She had called Cathy right before she went to bed but got no answer. She had texted, too, and left her voicemails, but she got no response. All Cathy had told Jeannie the morning of the opening was that Travis had slumped and she'd promptly rushed him to the hospital. She had later said that he had regained consciousness and that there was no cause for alarm, but Cathy was now unreachable. Jeannie was starting to worry.

"I'll stop by her house tomorrow if I still can't get through to her today," Jeannie said. "I don't want to jump the gun or worry over nothing, but...if I don't see her, I won't rest."

"Alright," Aaron said. "Let me know if you need anything, alright?"

"I will."

"Speaking of needs," Aaron continued and cleared his throat. "You need a car. I know your house isn't a long distance from the shop, but don't you think having a car will be more convenient for you? You will need to go to the market to shop and carry a lot of bags and groceries. It's only ideal."

"I don't know, Aaron. A car really isn't within my budget right now," Jeannie said.

"I have one wasting away in my garage," he said and shrugged. "I mean, you can have it if you want."

Jeannie stifled a smirk. She knew it was coming. It had gotten to the point where she could tell what Aaron wanted to say before he even said it. The man was doing too much, and not that she was complaining, but Jeannie's heart couldn't handle all the love she was receiving from him.

"It's fine," she said. "I don't think I need a car."

"I want you to have it," he insisted.

"And I don't want it," Jeannie said. "Aaron, you're doing too much."

"How is that a problem?" he asked.

"It burdens me. I don't do nearly half of what you do for me on a daily basis. How about we kick it down a notch? I am happy with your presence. Having you around is enough for me."

"Oh, come on."

Jeannie wasn't bluffing. Aaron's presence was a kind of comfort she had never experienced before. Being around him felt like a warm blanket or hot cocoa on a freezing cold day. He truly was enough for her.

"Aaron," Jeannie said quietly. "I don't need a car. If I did, you're the first person I'd tell. Well, I might tell Mason first, but still. I'll tell you. Don't worry about me. I am a grown woman, who might be a grandmother soon if Kelly would just get serious and get pregnant already."

Aaron gasped softly. "I would spoil that child."

"I have no doubt about that." Jeannie giggled.

"You know, I've not actually held a baby in decades. The only baby I've held in my arms is George, my brother," Aaron revealed. "But that was so long ago, I don't even remember what that feels like."

His statement broke Jeannie's heart. "It's not too late. You can do whatever you want to do."

They sat there in silence and finished the pot pie. A couple of minutes later, Aaron received a call from work, and it went on for about fifteen minutes while Jeannie sat there and listened in on the conversation. Aaron was different when he was on the phone. With her, his eyebrows were relaxed, his tone was quieter, and he seemed playful. But when he spoke on the phone, his eyebrows were always drawn in at the corners, his voice got deeper, and he was suddenly serious. Jeannie liked to watch him. It still fascinated her how she of all people had someone like Aaron by her side. He felt like a trophy that she'd won.

"Jeannie—"

"You have to go?"

Aaron dropped his shoulders. "I do. But I'll see you later. I'll stop by your house on my way home."

There was no use arguing, so Jeannie just nodded. "Alright. I'll see you later. Text me when you can."

"I will," Aaron said, pecked her on the cheek, and scurried out of the shop.

Jeannie put everything at the shop in order before closing for the day. She had decided to work Mondays through to Saturdays, from 8 a.m. to 8 p.m. Over time, she would employ more people, but Jeannie figured that it could wait until her plan was in full effect.

Soon, it was nighttime, and although Jeannie didn't think Aaron would make it to her house, she still made him dinner and waited. Usually, he claimed to have all the time in the world to spend with her, but when Aaron got to work, he practically buried himself in it. Still, Jeannie wanted to see Aaron, so she made him some pasta, opened a bottle of wine, and plated the dish on the kitchen counter. Then she proceeded to sit in the living room and read.

About ten minutes past ten o'clock, Jeannie heard a knock on the door. She paused and set her novel down. Usually,

Aaron tried to open the door before knocking. He always assumed the door was unlocked.

"Who is it?" Jeannie asked, standing up from the couch.

"It's me," she heard a familiar voice say.

Jeannie stifled a groan as she contemplated not opening the door. It had been a wonderful week of silence without Luka around. Now he was back.

Reluctantly, Jeannie opened the door. Her plan was simple. She'd pretend to be too tired to talk to him and ask that he came back tomorrow. However, on opening the door, Jeannie froze.

"Luka, what happened?" Jeannie asked, confused.

Luka stood there with tears rolling down his cheeks. He was visibly shaken by something, and his eyes were red. Immediately, Jeannie recalled why he'd left in the first place.

"Can I come in?" Luka asked, almost in a whisper. "Please?"

Jeannie nodded instinctively and shut the door behind her. "What happened? Did you come all the way here crying? What could be so—"

"I have three months to live, Jeannie," Luka announced and threw his hands in the air. "It's official. I am dying. Three months! Ninety days! I don't want to believe it. I can't. I mean, I knew I had cancer, but I didn't expect to be dying so soon. What am I going to do in 90 days, Jeannie? What's the use?"

Jeannie's heart dropped. She covered her mouth with her palm to muffle a gasp. "Luka, I am so sorry. Is that what the doctor said?"

Luka nodded. "According to him, I'd be bedridden soon. I need to start chemotherapy if I want a better chance at survival, and I have to prepare myself for whatever is to come. What am I supposed to do? Start writing my will? Saying goodbye?"

Jeannie took a step forward. "No, of course not. We know that cancer is pretty serious, but with the right treatment, you can live a longer life. Don't give up now, Luka."

"I am starting to feel it, Jeannie," Luka rasped with a quivering voice. "I can feel it. I'm not strong enough to handle this. This is karma for all I did to you and my children, and I know it. I was stupid. Every single time, I left thinking that when I returned, I'd be back with millions so we would never have to work again. But what's the use? Look at how I lived my life. I ruined it all. And I'm all alone. I am shaking in my boots, Jeannie. I don't want to die alone."

Jeannie moved even closer. "You're not alone," she heard herself say. "Remember I said I'd be the friend you need? I wasn't lying. I'll help you get through this. It's scary, and I understand that."

Luka broke down sobbing. "Oh, Jeannie. I don't know what I ever did to deserve your concern. You have the purest heart, and I might not be the best person, but I am grateful for you."

"It's alright. You'll get through this," Jeannie said. "Besides, you have to live for Lily. She has grown too fond of you, and you must not break her heart. I won't allow it. So live, Luka. Do your best to."

Luka nodded and wiped his tears. "Thank you," he whispered. "Do you mind if I stay here for a bit? I'll leave soon, I promise. I just don't want to be alone right now. I'm having too many bad thoughts and I'm afraid of what I might do with all this regret I'm feeling."

Jeannie instinctively embraced Luka and patted him on the back. "You will get through this. Just stay strong."

Luka in turn wrapped his arms around Jeannie's waist and pulled her closer to him. He sobbed into her shoulders as he held onto her tightly. Jeannie had never seen Luka like this. Never this vulnerable. Even when he was asking for her forgiveness, he never cried. He always maintained a silent form of smugness.

Perhaps she was too lost in her thoughts, but Jeannie didn't hear the door open.

"What in the world is going on here?" she heard Aaron rasp.

Swiftly, Jeannie spun around, and she could swear that her heart stopped beating. Aaron stood in front of them with a bouquet of flowers in his hands and a bewildered look on his face.

It then clicked for Jeannie. She finally understood what Cathy was saying about unfinished business.

Chapter Fifteen

oments before...
Aaron opened his eyes when the car came to a halt in front of Jeannie's house. He yawned and shook his head vigorously. At this point, he was barely surviving on five hours of sleep per night. He had a ton of work to do, but he could never seem to concentrate until he saw Jeannie. Hence, Aaron spent the day with his partner, and then worked for most of the night. At first, it didn't bother him, but seeing how he was constantly tired, he had to find time to actually rest.

"We've arrived, sir," the driver said.

Aaron glanced at Jeannie's house. "Right. Thank you for driving me on such short notice, Connor. I was just too tired to get behind the wheel. I promise I won't take too long. I just need to give someone these flowers and we'll be on our way."

"No problem, sir. I'm happy to wait."

"Thank you," Aaron replied.

He was about to step out of the car when his phone buzzed in his pocket. Aaron paused and pulled it out to answer.

"I'm sorry for calling so late, Mr. Horn," the voice from the other end said.

Aaron's eyebrows furrowed and he slammed his head on the dash. He knew why Daniel, one of his regional managers in Seattle, was calling him so late. For weeks, he had been trying to set up a meeting with Aaron.

"It's alright, Daniel," Aaron said. "Are you calling for the same reason?"

"I'm afraid I am, sir," Daniel answered. "Mr. Horn, the client is tired of virtual meetings with you. It's a huge deal, and dealing over the phone won't suffice. We need to sit down together and discuss the agreements before we proceed. I know you're going to ask that Matilda handles the discussions, but they insist on dealing with you directly. We need you here in Seattle to close the deal. Matilda can't do it."

"I was just hoping to sign the documents when you all reach an agreement," Aaron said. "That's why I formed a team over there. I assumed you'd be capable enough to convince the client to deal with us. I have a lot to do here in Chickadee Cove. I can't leave."

By a lot, Aaron meant Jeannie. If he could convince her to accompany him to Seattle, he would, but knowing Jeannie, she would disagree. The bakery just opened, and it would be insane to ask her to travel with him. Still, Aaron couldn't leave her side. He didn't want to. Not when her ex-husband was roaming the streets of Chickadee Cove, looking for a way back into her life. Aaron had no idea what his intentions were, but it couldn't be anything good.

"It's one meeting, sir," Daniel tried to persuade him. "You don't even have to be here for an entire day. You can fly into the state and be out once the meeting is over. I think this client are fans of you, which is why they are insisting that they deal with you directly."

"Fine," Aaron said. "I'll handle it. I'll call them, schedule a meeting, and be in Seattle within the week. Get all the documents ready. I don't want any delay on this. Get all the papers, taxes, and all the other things ready, too. If this client wants to see me, then I assume they don't intend to waste my time."

"Thank you, sir. We'll get everything ready."

Aaron ended the call and exhaled. He was left with no choice. Leaving Chickadee Cove was the last thing he wanted to do, but Aaron reckoned he'd be back in no time, at least before Luka returned from wherever he'd disappeared to.

Jeannie had no idea that Aaron knew about her meetings with Luka. He had heard of Luka meeting her at the shop and coming to her house, and how Luka was going around town telling anyone who would listen that he and Jeannie were "working things out." Of course, it angered Aaron, but he trusted Jeannie when she said she'd handle it. Given all she had said about Luka, there was no way she was taking him back after all he'd done.

"Sir, are you alright?" Conner asked, turning to stare at Aaron.

"Yes," he answered. "Keep the engine running. I'll be back soon."

Aaron groaned as he exited the vehicle. Seeing Jeannie was going to take all the pain away, and he knew it. That was why he was there. Aaron couldn't explain it, but Jeannie's presence made a lot of difference in his mood. Ever since the very first day he laid eyes on her she'd been like a breath of a different, fresher air than he was used to. They had something special going on for them, and Aaron was sure Jeannie felt it, too. He had never been so sure about someone in his entire life.

Without sparing a second to knock, Aaron opened the door and stepped into the room. He first got a whiff of that familiar, rosy scent of Jeannie's living room and a smile instinctively formed on his face. Perhaps it was better to ask

Conner to take the car home. Aaron decided he was going to spend the night. What better place to get a good night's rest?

That smile that had formed on Aaron's lips a second ago slowly started to wane when his eyes set on the image before him. At first, Aaron was convinced that he was hallucinating. It was the lack of sleep. That had to be the reason he was imagining his worst nightmare. There was absolutely no way that Luka was in Jeannie's living room with his arms tightly wrapped around his woman. There was no possible way.

To confirm that Aaron was actually living his nightmare, Luka lifted his head up, paused his crying, and the right corner of his lips rose.

"What in the world is going on here?" Aaron rasped. "Am I dreaming right now?"

"Aaron," Jeannie breathed. "You came."

"What? You didn't think I'd come? Is that why this is happening?"

Luka still had that smug look on his face and it made Aaron's blood boil. Was he mocking him? Trying to assert dominance? Trying to tell Aaron that he had no place there? That he had Jeannie wrapped around his finger? The look on Luka's face angered Aaron, but what drove him to the edge was Luka's hands still wrapped firmly around Jeannie's waist.

In a fit of rage, Aaron charged for Luka and shoved him away from Jeannie's side. Luka staggered back and hit the kitchen counter. He groaned and held his head.

"Aaron!" Jeannie yelled.

Behind them were two plates of food and an open bottle of wine. Aaron scoffed. Jeannie always talked about not wanting to be in Luka's presence anymore. She claimed she had control of things, and that she wasn't interested in her ex-husband, but there she was, having dinner with him.

Aaron felt weak all of a sudden. "What did I do to be

treated this way, Jeannie? Name one thing I did wrong. I didn't ask for much, did I? All I wanted was for this to not happen. For your sake, and for our relationship. If you don't respect me, at least respect our relationship. What is this? You're having dinner with him? In your house? This late? Was he not planning on going home? He was going to spend the night?"

Before Jeannie could reply, Luka appeared again and shoved Aaron. He didn't stop. He continued to shove him, pushing him further toward the door.

"Who do you think you are?" Luka kept saying. "Who are you to talk to Jeannie like that?"'

The audacity of the man. Aaron tried his best to keep his cool, but that face...that look...the nerve.

It was driving him insane.

Aaron clenched his fist and punched Luka so hard that he went straight to the ground. He didn't think it through, and if he had taken the time to get his emotions in check, he wouldn't have reacted that way. But Luka was practically asking for it.

"Luka!" Jeannie screamed, rushing to the ground. "Are you alright? Are you bleeding?"

Aaron couldn't believe his eyes. No. It all had to be a dream. He didn't want to believe that Jeannie—his Jeannie—had her hands on Luka's face and was assessing him for injuries while he was standing there.

"Why would you do that?" Jeannie lashed at him, red with rage. "Why hit him?"

Aaron squinted his eyes. "Are you—did you see him attack me? Did you see him shove me?"

"You shoved first!" she yelled. "He's sick. I told you he's sick and you go ahead and punch him? What kind of man are you? Hitting a sick person? His lip is bleeding."

"I think he broke my jaw," Luka said almost inaudibly. "I

can hear ringing. Please help me to my feet, Jeannie. My back hurts."

Jeannie shook her head in disappointment and returned to Luka's side. She held him by the waist as he struggled to his feet. Luka in turn had his hand over Jeannie's shoulder. Once he was on his feet, his hand travelled to her back, and he fixed his gaze on Aaron with that same smug smirk still on his face. It disgusted Aaron to see Jeannie like that. So easy to manipulate.

"You know what?" Aaron asked. "You both deserve each other. I shouldn't be here. In fact, I should have taken the hint weeks ago when you asked me to leave in the middle of my proposal. Take care of your sick husband, Jeannie. I'm sure he's a changed man."

Aaron dropped the bouquet of flowers on the ground and walked out of the house. He had so much rage inside that he felt like punching the wall, but he managed to keep his cool even as he got into his car.

"Home?" Conner asked.

"A bar," Aaron responded through clenched teeth. "Take me to a bar or something, please."

"Alright," he answered and pulled into the road.

Aaron reached into his pocket, whipped out his phone, and dialed Mason's number. Out of everyone in his life that he could think of to call in that moment, Mason was the only one on his mind. He had grown closer to him, and the thought that all of that could end because of Jeannie's naivety saddened him.

"Aaron," Mason said through the phone. "My game isn't until tomorrow."

"Oh, I know," Aaron answered. "I didn't call to wish you luck, I called about your mother."

"Oh, is she alright?" Mason asked with a worried tone in his voice.

Aaron sighed. "Honestly, I cannot answer that question properly. Physically, she's alright. But I called because your mother and I won't be seeing each other for now. I wanted to tell you this first. Honestly, it's not how I'd like things to be, but that's how they are. I'm tired, I'm drained, I'm hurt, I'm embarrassed, and I can't think."

Mason took a while to respond. "It's Luka, isn't it? He's finally found his way back."

"Well, it's your mother. She cannot be that naïve. I cannot understand how she—" Aaron swallowed and sighed. "I don't know what's going through her head, but I think we need space for her to sort it out. She wants to be by his side, and I cannot stop her. But I also cannot be by her side while she does it."

"I'm so sorry, Aaron. I'm sorry about all of this."

"There's nothing to be sorry about," Aaron answered. "It's her life. Her choices. I called you for another reason. It's shameless of me to ask this, but even though your mother and I might not be together right now, I'd still like to call you and talk to you like we always do. I don't want that to change."

"Absolutely. Neither do I," Mason said. "Plus, this isn't your problem, Aaron. I know you have good intentions with our mother, but she has a problem that she needs to figure out. It's not on you to do that for her, it's on us, her children. Actually, Emily and I have been working on something to ensure that she doesn't make the same mistakes again, and we won't rest until we find a way to get her out of this. We were there all these years, so we can talk sense into her. We'll speak to her. Mom thinks she's doing the right thing...the human thing, but that's just nonsense. I think it's high time we take this more seriously before she ruins all the good things in her life again."

"Help her, Mason," Aaron said. "Your father might be sick, but that doesn't make him a good person. Sooner or later, Jeannie will get hurt. I could see it in Luka's eyes. I don't know what he wants or why he feels possessive of Jeannie, but it's not good. He doesn't look like a good person, and I am not saying this because I love your mother, I mean it from the bottom of my heart."

"Oh, we know. We know him. Mom claims to know him best, but she's blind. Let us handle it. I'll call Emily and Kelly, we'll make some calls and figure out a way to save my mother from herself before she self-destructs. Thank you, Aaron."

"No problem. Good luck at your game tomorrow. I'll be watching it," Aaron said.

"Bye, Aaron."

Aaron set the phone down and shut his eyes. He had tried all that he could, but at this junction, he was ready to give up and let fate just take its course. Ever since he had met Jeannie, all he'd done was imagine different scenarios with her as his wife. He wanted to do all that he couldn't do in his previous marriage with her. Perhaps Jeannie was meant to just pass through his life. Maybe she and Luka were the ones meant to be. Maybe he was just wasting his time.

It hurt more to think that she might have been playing with his feelings. Did she care about him at all? If she did, then why was she having dinner with someone she told him not to worry about? Why did she defend that man? Why didn't she take his side? Why has she never taken his side?

Aaron's phone buzzed again, and he picked it up swiftly, hoping that Jeannie was the one calling. His heart sank when he saw an unfamiliar number displayed on the screen.

"Hello?" Aaron said lazily. "Who's this?"

"Aaron. Hey. It's me, Isabel."

Chapter Sixteen

Jeannie wiped a tear from her cheek and dialed Aaron's number again. It had been three days. Three whole days since the incident, and he wasn't taking her calls. She had been to his house twice, but he wasn't home. He wasn't at the sawmill, either. His employees weren't allowed to say where he was, so Jeannie couldn't get information from them. It was almost as if he had vanished into thin air.

Deep down, Jeannie had no idea why she was searching so hard for Aaron. She didn't have the confidence to apologize, and she was almost certain he'd never forgive her and that she couldn't give him what he wanted. She couldn't give anyone what they wanted. They all wanted Luka gone, but Jeannie couldn't send him away. What then was the use in reconciling with Aaron if she was still going to be friends with Luka?

Still, she wanted to see him. Even if it was only a glimpse. What if he was sick again? Or the stress had gotten to him? Jeannie was so worried about feeling guilty if Luka happened to die that she didn't realize she'd hate herself if she saw Aaron in the hospital again.

She sat in the waiting room at Hope Hospital together

with Cathy. Travis was still sick, and the doctors claimed he had a rare heart condition. They were still running tests, but Cathy wasn't doing so well with the news. Jeannie had visited to keep her company, but she had ulterior motives when she was on her way to the hospital. Thankfully, Aaron wasn't admitted there like the last time, which meant that he wasn't sick again.

But where could he be?

"You're thinking about Aaron, aren't you?" Cathy asked. Her voice was weak, and her eyes were puffy.

"Cathy, we don't need to talk about that now," Jeannie told her. "Your child is the priority. Worry about him."

"I need to distract myself," she said. "What I was trying to say is that you shouldn't be thinking of Aaron."

Jeannie turned to her friend. "Why not?"

"Because you don't deserve to. You made your choice, stick to it."

Jeannie felt tears sting her eyes. "Can you at least be nice to me?" she asked with a trembling voice. "I can't help who I am. I'm only trying to help someone, and everyone is making it seem as though I'm the one committing a crime when I've done nothing wrong. He has three months to live. Why is everyone so harsh?"

Cathy sniffed and placed her head against the wall. "Jeannie. Imagine this with me. A thief comes into your house. They take everything. They take your bed, your furniture, your television, all your money. Every single thing. They leave you with nothing but trauma. You manage to buy some furniture back, and a bigger television. Then, later on, after squandering everything you had, they return. He tells you that he needs a roof over his head. He's sick, and he might die soon. You know he steals, and you just bought some stuff with all the money you had left. Will you still let him in, knowing that he is very likely to steal from you again?"

"It's not the same thing," Jeannie whispered. "You know who Luka was to me before we even started dating in high school. We were friends first. We should have just stayed friends. But we dated, and that ruined everything. I'm not looking to be romantically involved with Luka ever again, but no one has told me why we can't stay friends, especially now that he really needs one."

Cathy rubbed her face roughly with her palm. "Jeannie, I am going through a lot right now, so I'm just going to be blunt with you. I'm not going to sugarcoat anything."

Jeannie nodded. "Go ahead."

"You don't listen," Cathy started. "How many times have we been over this? How many times have we talked about Luka? Name one good thing his presence has done for you. One. You can't, can you? You're a good person, kind and helpful, but you have a deep problem, my friend. You're stubborn and naïve. Like a child. When Travis first touched a hotplate, he learned never to do so again. Even when the hotplate was cold, he would never touch it, even though it couldn't hurt him. Learn from that. I have said it, Mason has said it, Emily and Kelly have said it, and I will say it again. The fact that Luka is sick does not give him access to your life again. My goodness. He might be sick, but he is still Luka. The same man who might be the cause of Lily's current problems. He is the same person, only he has cancer. Nothing has changed. Luka is Luka. Draw a boundary before it's too late. Get him a nurse, get him someone to help him. It shouldn't be you."

"Cathy—"

"This is the last time I will be talking about Luka, Jeannie," Cathy said. "If you ever mention him again, I'll ignore you. Luka was a problem two years ago, and because of you, I have to put up with him. I am angry at Luka because of you. Because of what he did to you, but you—"

Cathy lifted her head to the ceiling and inhaled deeply. "Do what you want to do, Jeannie. You don't listen to me anyway."

Jeannie brushed her hair with her fingers, fighting back the tears. "What do I do about Aaron, Cathy? He's not answering his phone, he won't speak to me, and it's killing me. I don't know what to do."

Cathy stared at her. "Remember what I said about unfinished business?"

"That they take care of themselves?" Jeannie whispered.

Cathy nodded. "It just did. You did nothing about it, and it took care of itself."

"Cathy, come on. Can you please call him? Maybe he'll answer if it's you."

"What are you even going to say to him?" Cathy asked. "That you're sorry for taking Luka's side? You've already apologized for that in the past. But you did it again. What are you going to say this time?"

"I don't know," Jeannie said.

"For anything to work right now, you need Luka gone. From the look of things, it'll be difficult for you to do that. I would have helped to tell him off, but he won't listen to me. It has to come from you. So, whenever you're ready, whenever you feel like you've had enough of him, get your freedom back and then approach Aaron. You can't have your cake and eat it."

"I just want to talk to him," Jeannie said.

Cathy threw her hand in the air. "Well, put yourself in his shoes. How would you feel if you saw Aaron having dinner with his ex-girlfriend, at his house, at ten at night?"

"I wasn't having dinner with him," Jeannie said, frustrated. "The dinner was for Aaron. I was upset, and I overreacted, I admit to it. Aaron did not deserve me yelling at his face. But he hit Luka, and you know how Aaron is built. How strong he is. I thought the punch was going to kill him."

"Is that such a bad thing?" Cathy said dryly.

"Cathy, I'm being serious here," Jeannie whined. "Tell me what to do."

"Look, my dear," Cathy started. "You know I love you, and I will do anything for you. But for my sake, and my mental health, I don't want to talk about Luka anymore. It's absurd and I sound like a broken record at this point. I'm sure you'll figure it out."

Jeannie had more to say, but she decided to keep it to herself. Cathy already had a lot on her plate with Travis, and she didn't want to add to her friend's burden. Besides, her stand in the matter was clear and unwavering.

"How's the bakery?" Cathy asked, changing the subject. "With you so distracted, how are you running the place?"

"Baking helps clear my mind, so the bakery is fine," Jeannie answered. "I get there very early every day, bake the items on our menu, and then leave because the place reminds me too much of Aaron. I don't know what I was thinking, Cathy. Aaron probably hates me now for not taking his side."

"I wouldn't be surprised," Cathy mumbled.

"Cathy—"

"I'm joking," Cathy groaned. "He'll come around. Eventually."

After an hour passed, Jeannie decided to take her leave. She promised to return later that evening with some pastries for Cathy and Travis before making her way out of the hospital.

"Jeannie," a voice startled her as she walked down the hallway.

Jeannie turned around and almost immediately, it felt like a dark cloud was hovering over her head. Jeannie stared at

Luka and wondered how long she was going to let him put a hold on her life.

"I'm sorry, I shouldn't have come without telling you," Luka apologized. "I just...I know how much you love Cathy, and I wanted to make sure you were okay. After the incident at your place with that man, you and I haven't talked."

"I've been busy," Jeannie answered.

"I figured. You have a bakery to run." Luka nodded. "How's Cathy's son? I heard he's sick."

"We don't know yet. The doctors still want to run some tests, so we're waiting for results to come in. But he's talking and laughing, too. Hopefully, it's nothing to worry about."

"Hopefully," he said. "I also came over to ask you for a favor, Jeannie. That's if you don't mind."

"What is it?" Jeannie asked unenthusiastically.

"I need to go shopping," Luka explained. "Grocery shopping. I contemplated asking this several times, and you can totally say no, but...would you please go grocery shopping with me? I don't feel too well, and I haven't had good food in days. I'd like to cook something to eat, so I need ingredients."

"Luka, I can't. I'm sorry," Jeannie said.

Luka appeared shocked. "Why? I promise I won't take up all your time. I understand that you need to get back to the shop, too, so I will hurry. I wouldn't ask you to do this if I could do it alone. I just feel really lightheaded, and my hands are shaking. Please."

"Luka, it doesn't look good," Jeannie explained. "People will see us and make a big deal out of nothing. I think you should go home. Just text me what you need, and I'll get them for you."

"That's not fair to you, or to me," Luka said. "What could people possibly think? Most people here don't recognize me, so you could say I'm new in town. You're just helping me out. I could print it on a shirt and wear it. Just so everyone can see that you're only helping a friend out. Nothing more to it. Please. Just grocery shopping."

Jeannie sighed and scanned the hallway. "Just grocery shopping?"

"Yes. I won't take up a lot of your time."

"Alright, then. I guess I can accompany you," Jeannie finally agreed.

They headed out of the hospital, walking side by side. The supermarket was only a stone's throw from the hospital, so it was easy to walk over there.

"When are you going to the hospital, Luka?" Jeannie asked him as they walked. "Don't you think it's high time you started chemotherapy? You need to start treatment immediately if you want a good chance of fighting this. But I don't see you making any appointments with the doctors here at Hope Hospital. It's the best in Chickadee Cove."

Luke massaged his nape. "I'm not ready, Jeannie. I know that when I eventually start, my situation will get real. Like, it's actually happening. I don't want to face it yet. Plus, I do have a doctor. I speak to him almost every day over the phone. He wants me to return to New York soon, so we can get started on treatment, but I haven't actually made up by mind to go. Chemotherapy is painful, and before I start any treatment, I at least want to make amends with everyone I've ever offended. That list is small. You and my children. Once I do that, I'll be ready to face anything."

Jeannie had no idea what to say to it. Luka was adamant, and from the look of things, he wasn't planning on leaving her alone until he got his way. Jeannie, on the other hand, was not planning on giving Luka what he wanted, mainly because she had given her heart to someone else. But if she couldn't get Luka to understand that on time, then she was in for a long ride with Luka.

"Will you come to New York with me?" Luka chuckled. "I

already know the answer to that question, so there's no need for you to say anything. But, instead of New York, I'm thinking of getting treatment here instead. That way I have you closer to me."

"Luka, I don't want you relying on me for everything," Jeannie said. "I promised that I was going to help, but that doesn't mean our past is forgotten. I don't want to give you any false hopes about us, and I really hope you're not trying to use your illness to your advantage. I won't budge, what's done is done. I hope you understand that."

"You always say that, Jeannie," Luka responded. "Every time."

Jeannie paused abruptly and her eyebrows furrowed. "Are you mocking me?"

"What? Of course not," Luka stammered. "I would never. Forget I said anything. I'm sorry. Let's just shop. I'll be quiet."

Jeannie pinched the corners of her eyes and sighed. She had brought it on herself, and she had no right to complain. Given how poorly she'd handled the situation with Luka and Aaron, she wasn't surprised that Luka was convinced they'd be a couple again. If only she had deescalated the situation better. Instead, she let her emotions get the best of her and she'd snapped at Aaron, of all people. He didn't deserve it.

They got the shopping cart and began to stroll down each aisle, searching for the groceries Luka needed. Jeannie was pushing the cart, but her mind was everywhere else. She would rather be anywhere else. But since it was almost impossible for her to say no, she had to deal with the consequences of her own actions. She wanted to be a good person, but it didn't feel right to be a good person to Luka.

"Oh no. Not again," Luka sighed.

Jeannie lifted her head, and she practically froze solid when she saw Aaron standing in front of them with a shopping basket in his hand. He looked at her, at Luka, and then back at her.

"Aaron," Jeannie blurted. "I was worried. I called you several times, and—"

"Why were you calling?" Aaron asked with a husky tone.

"Jenny, if he touches me again, I'll sue. You see the way he's looking at me, right?" Luka chipped in. "Do you know how much pain you put me in because of your temper?"

Aaron looked so disappointed, and it broke Jeannie's heart to pieces. An apology would do nothing to make things any better. There she was, standing side by side with the very cause of the issue. He was never going to listen.

Without uttering another word, Aaron walked past them. Jeannie watched him leave the aisle without looking back at her. He looked done. Finally over her mistakes. Who could blame him? Even she didn't know what she was doing with herself.

Chapter Seventeen

It was Sunday. Jeannie was indifferent about leaving her house that morning, but if she remained in bed, she was going to cry. Again. Attending church was the best way to distract herself from how utterly disoriented her life had become.

In the space of one week after her bakery opened, Jeannie had lost the will to do anything. She was like a walking corpse. Without Aaron's calls, visits, text messages, or the sound of his voice, Jeannie didn't feel like herself anymore. Time passed slowly, and she would wake up at night to cry.

It wasn't just Aaron. It seemed everyone else had abandoned her, too. Jeannie felt alone. Cathy was at the hospital with her son. She tried her best to call and check up on Jeannie, but there wasn't much that she could do to help. Mason was busy with the season, and he could barely call. Kelly was in another country enjoying her prolonged honeymoon, and Jeannie hated to disturb her. Emily wasn't speaking to her. At least, not like she used to. And Lily, well... Jeannie would rather call anyone else.

Nothing was working.

Except Luka. That man was working hard. He didn't take no for an answer, and Jeannie was either too weak to argue with him or she felt sorry for his situation. He'd come by the bakery, help clean, and attend to customers. He'd walk Jeannie home, and even the times she stood her ground and protested, he'd follow closely behind her like a stalker. He thought it was a cute thing to do, the little things, but it burdened Jeannie. She didn't want him around all the time because people were bound to start rumors, but he'd always play the cancer card and she'd shut up.

Like a pushover.

After spending about two hours getting dressed for church, Jeannie took her bag and walked out of the house.

"Good morning, sunshine. I figured you'd be going to church this morning."

Jeannie held the key in the keyhole as she contemplated running back into the house. He was doing it on purpose. He had to be tormenting her on purpose.

"Luka, please," Jeannie whispered and then turned around to find him standing there with a bright smile on his face. "Are you sure you're sick? You are everywhere. When do you rest?"

He chuckled lightly. "What do you mean? I'm just always happy to see you. I like being around you."

"I didn't sign up for this," Jeannie whispered again. "I didn't sign up to see you every day. Sometimes I prefer to be alone. Like today. It's Sunday, for heaven's sake. You should be resting, or planning your trip to the hospital, because frankly, I don't understand why you are not in the hospital. You don't look too good."

"I'm planning the trip," he said. "That's why I like being around you all the time. Who knows when next I'll see you after I leave? I'm only trying to enjoy these little moments."

Jeannie exhaled. "Fine. Are you headed to church?"

"I am," he said, nodding. "I figured I need to confess my

sins and beg God for a second chance at life. I haven't been to church in a while, and I don't know anyone here in Chickadee Cove. That's another reason I came. I was hoping we could go together."

Jeannie walked down the short stairs and placed her key in her bag. "Let's go."

"I'll drive," Luka offered, gesturing at his car. "Let's go."

"No. I'd rather walk," she answered. "It's a short distance, and I need the fresh air to clear my head."

"But Jenny—"

"Don't argue with me, Luka. Please. I'd really like to walk. You can drive behind me if you want, or I could give you directions."

"Okay," Luka said and raised both hands. "We'll walk."

They strolled down the street in silence. Jeannie really needed the walk, but she also didn't want to arrive at the crowded church in Luka's car. There were enough rumors going around the town about her already.

"Are you serious, Jeannie?" were the first words Cathy said to her as soon as they arrived at the gate.

"Cathy Lucas," Luka said, standing behind Jeannie. "We didn't get to say hello properly the last time."

Cathy finally made eye contact with Luka. "If you haven't figured it out by now, Luka, I'm not going to be nice to you just because you're sick like Jeannie is doing. Unlike her, I don't pretend. I tell things as they are. You're not a good person, and I can boldly say this because I know the hell you put your children and Jeannie through. You have no right to be here, and if you had any shame, you'd leave her alone."

"Ouch," Luka voiced. "I haven't seen you in decades, and you think you know me? It hurts me how much you lot disrespect Jeannie. What do you mean 'unlike her'? You're calling Jeannie a pretender? It looks like you don't know Jeannie after all because she's nothing like that."

Cathy scoffed. "You think I don't know what you're doing? Do you really think I'm that stupid? You are a serial cheat, a liar, and this is all a game to you. She might not see that because she chooses to believe that there is good in everyone, but I see through your lies. You came here knowingly to use your illness to your advantage. All you need is the right platform and you'd be a sociopathic killer, too."

"I will not stand here and listen to you spit hurtful words at me," Luka rasped. "I'm trying, here. You're just a stuck-up woman who won't mind her own business."

"Cathy is on the edge," Jeannie chimed in. "She's going through a lot right now, so please don't agitate her more than she already is."

Cathy scoffed. "I'm on the edge? Really, Jeannie? You're trying to make him understand why I'm furious with him? And your excuse is that I'm on the edge?"

"I'm not trying to make him understand anything, I was just saying," Jeannie tried to defend herself.

"Do you always pick a fight with her?" Luka asked Cathy. "No wonder Jeannie is always uneasy."

"You think she's uneasy because of me?" Cathy argued. "It's you. She can't tell you because she's a pushover, but it's you. Her life would be so much better if you just leave her alone."

Luka squinted his eyes. "Did you just call Jeannie a pushover? Are you kidding me? How do you speak of her like that?"

Jeannie stared into space as they exchanged words in front of the church. It was incredibly embarrassing, but she couldn't just walk away. That would disrespect them both, and Cathy would be even more pissed at her.

Cathy was right. She was a pushover, and she had accepted it. It was embarrassing that after all these years she still found it hard to stand her ground. Seeing how Cathy was so quick to speak up and put Luka in his place made Jeannie envy her. She could never do that. The years of suffering were supposed to give her a tough skin, but instead, she'd become even softer.

"Enough," Jeannie finally said. "Please. Both of you. We're in front of a church. People are watching us."

"People are watching you," Cathy said. "I came here to pray to God for my son to be alright. But now I'm angry. I came here for peace, and you brought him here."

"It's a church," Luka said. "How can you be so judgmental and expect your prayers to be answered? Didn't the bible tell you judge not, lest ye be judged?"

"I'm not judging you," Cathy said. "I'm telling you what you are. A liar, and a cheat. You might deserve a second chance with God, but you do not deserve a second chance with Jeannie. I will not rest until she sees it and finally stands up for herself because I know you're shameless, and you will not leave until Jeannie dismisses you. But she can't do that because she feels sorry for you."

"That's what makes her a better, more mature person than you'll ever be," Luka lashed at her.

Cathy turned to Jeannie. "I'm not sitting with him. Not on the same row, the same aisle. If you sit with him, that's up to you. I'll see you after church, and we will have a long talk about this thing you're doing."

"Cathy," Jeannie called out to her and held her hand firmly. "Don't abandon me, too. I'm begging you. Right now, you are the only person that I can talk to."

Cathy clicked her tongue. "Why are you torturing yourself then? You're doing this to yourself. You know that, right?"

Jeannie pulled Cathy a few feet away from Luka. "He's leaving soon for treatment in New York. I just have to wait till then."

"You don't have to do anything," Cathy said. "No one is forcing you to be the perfect human being. This isn't right.

Does it feel right to you? Coming to church with him? You could have come separately."

"I just need some time, alright? Honestly, I'm not handling this split with Aaron well. I'm not alright, and I can't think straight. I couldn't care less what Luka is doing, and I don't have the strength to argue with him or anyone. I don't feel like doing anything. I think I'm broken. It's serious. I stopped having headaches when Aaron and I starting officially seeing each other, but now my headaches are back. I had an apple for lunch yesterday and I haven't eaten anything since because I don't feel like it. Mason is busy, Emily won't talk to me, I don't want to disturb Kelly, and if I talk to Lily, she'll just annoy me. I know I have made mistakes, and I am still making them, but give me time to do this. This isn't a forever thing. It's only until he gets better."

Cathy gave Jeannie a sorry look, then proceeded to hug her. "Goodness gracious. You're a mess, and it's all Luka's fault. Again. I understand what you're feeling, Jeannie, but you won't get better with him around. I hope you know that. So, pray hard today. Pray to God that Luka gets better fast so your life can go back to the way it was."

"It looks like lover boy moved on fast," Luka voiced, interrupting their conversation.

Jeannie pulled away from Cathy's embrace and followed Luka's gaze. She quickly spotted Aaron's car, and getting out were Aaron and Isabel. Jeannie must have been staring too intensely, because Aaron's gaze soon met hers. If he'd held her gaze for a little bit longer, Jeannie would have scurried to his side to talk to him, but Aaron looked away. He waved at Cathy instead, who waved back, and then he proceeded into the church with Isabel following closely behind him.

"They look perfect together," Luka noted. "I might not like the guy, but I do have to admit that he's good-looking. But man is he aggressive."

"You provoked him," Jeannie said to Luka, glaring at him. "It's your fault he's not talking to me."

"Look who's finally talking," Cathy mumbled.

"Jeannie, he revealed his true colors," Luka said. "There's no way you'd want to be with someone with so much rage inside. You've known me for years. Have I ever reacted that way to anything? People like him are bad news. Trust me. I'm a man. I know."

"What are your true colors, Luka Smith?" Cathy asked him, tilting her head to the side. "I bet they are far worse than his are."

"You're bitter," Luka said to her. "Heal."

Jeannie stormed into the church and sat on the other side, far away from Aaron but close enough to observe him from behind. Soon after, Cathy walked in, too, and sat by her side. Then Luka followed and sat on her other side. Jeannie could feel her heart pounding in her chest. After so many days, she was feeling something other than regret.

Jealousy.

She glared at the back of Isabel's head and couldn't stop her face from morphing into a scowl. Jeannie was convinced that Isabel had taken advantage of Aaron's vulnerability. She had seen an opening, and she had jumped on it.

"You know what you're feeling right now?" Cathy whispered in Jeannie's ear. "That's exactly what Aaron has been feeling seeing you and Luka frolicking around town. You have no right to be mad, actually. You're here with Luka, aren't you?"

Jeannie turned to glare at Luka. She wanted to ask him to sit somewhere else, but it would sound mean. The chances of her reconciling with Aaron were getting slimmer and slimmer by the day. If she did manage to get rid of Luka in the end, how was she going to get Isabel away from Aaron?

Church service ended sooner than Jeannie expected. She

had barely paid attention because she'd been too busy staring at Aaron and Isabel. All through the service, Isabel had not stopped touching Aaron or whispering into his ear whilst giggling playfully.

"Aren't you leaving?" Cathy asked her as people started to rise to their feet.

"Aaron hasn't gotten up from his seat yet," Jeannie answered, watching him.

"So?"

"I want to talk to him."

"If you want to talk to him, go over there."

"Isabel's there."

Cathy rolled her eyes. "Again, I ask, so?"

Just then, Aaron rose to his feet, and Jeannie instinctively stood up, too. She hesitated as she watched him walk down the aisle alone. She secretly hoped that he was coming toward her. That he'd look at her. If he did, she'd take it as a cue to approach him.

Sadly, Aaron walked out of the church without sparing a glance at her. Jeannie drew in a shaky breath and dropped her head. She should have approached him first.

"So, what are you going to do now?" Cathy asked her.

"Cry," Jeannie answered. "I'm going home to have a good cry."

Chapter Eighteen

Two days later...

"You are sure you all can handle the shop without me here?"

Sarah, one of the bakers and second-in-command at the bakery, nodded. "We'll survive. You don't look so well. Go home. If we need anything, we'll make sure to call you."

"I can stay for a bit," Jeannie insisted. "I just...I won't work, I'll just sit in the corner and watch you all. So, if there's anything you need, I'll be here to help."

Sarah squatted by Jeannie's side. She had her afro tucked into a blue hair net, and her apron was covered in flour.

"We don't need your help, Jeannie," Sarah said. "We might have been working here for only a week, but we got this. You've taught us the recipes, and we're already done making the pastries for today. All that's left is to prep for tomorrow. Go home. We are your employees for a reason. Why stress yourself when you have us?"

"You look like you're about to pass out," Denice, the other baker, said. "We can't have that. We might know the recipe, but we can't make it like you do. So go home and rest. You look like you haven't slept in days."

They were not wrong. Jeannie could barely keep her eyes open. She could barely control her head, and her chest was hurting. It had been hurting for days. She needed to rest. Baking was a distraction from her daily life, but ignoring her problems wasn't the solution. It wasn't going away until she fixed it herself. And by her problems, she meant her split with Aaron.

"Can I ask you both a question?" Jeannie said lazily.

"Sure," Denice answered as she peeled tangerines and juiced them.

"Let's say you have a partner," Jeannie started. "And you do something that hurts them. You break their heart. But you didn't mean to, you weren't thinking straight. The issue is, you made the same mistake twice, and this time, they decide they have had enough. They distance themselves from you and refuse to even look at you. You know that apologizing will do nothing. What do you do to let them know that you are sorry for disappointing them yet again?"

Denice and Sarah exchanged looks. "You stop disappointing them," Denice said and shrugged her shoulders. "It's that simple."

"I mean, in a case like that, an apology won't cut it," Sarah added. "Actions will speak louder. Not words. Let them know that you are not going to disappoint them again, and then you try not to. That's the only way to fix a problem like the one you described. But you still have to apologize. It's just the basic thing to do."

Everyone was saying the same thing, and Jeannie was convinced that there was no other way out of the situation. It all centered around Luka's disappearance from her life. As long as he was there, things were going to remain the same.

Jeannie said goodbye to all of them and left the shop in

their care. She made her way home, walking as slowly as possible. On one hand, she really needed to sleep. On the other hand, she didn't want to be alone at home. Her intrusive thoughts were hurtful, and if she dwelled on them, she wouldn't get any sleep.

Her other option was to visit Cathy at the hospital. But Jeannie knew they'd only end up arguing about Luka, and it would ruin both their moods. Her best bet was to go home, drink a lot of milk, and hope that sleep came faster than the intrusive thoughts.

As she strolled down the street, Jeannie thought about what Sarah had said. The basic thing to do was apologize even though it wasn't going to fix anything. The main issue was, Jeannie was absolutely sure she couldn't talk to Aaron without breaking down into tears. She didn't want him to feel burdened by her.

Still, she pulled out her phone from her back pocket and dialed his number. He was not going to answer, and that was fine. Jeannie wanted to leave a voicemail instead. That way, she could end it when she was at the verge of tears.

"Hey, it's Aaron. I'm sorry you can't reach me right now, but you know what to do after the beep."

"Hi, Aaron," Jeannie started. "I uh...I don't even know why I decided to leave you a message out of the blue, but I haven't spoken to you in over a week, and if I'm being totally honest with myself, it's killing me. I totally deserve this silent treatment from you, and I'm not complaining. However, I want to apologize. I was wrong. I've done it twice now. I always get angry at you and it's not right. If I should be angry at anyone, then it should be myself. Because I'm the biggest idiot. But, Aaron, I can't help how I am. I'm trying to put myself first, but it's hard to when you've lived all of your adult life caring for other people. I don't like feeling guilty, and all this while, I've been trying to avoid the guilt that might come with Luka possibly dying if I turn him away. I didn't realize how guilty I'd feel losing you over something that could have been avoided if I had been honest with you from the start. I said I was going to handle it, but I can't. I don't know how. It's not that I enjoy being easily accessible, it's that I cannot help it. What I do know is that I love you, and that I've never loved anyone like this before. And I don't want to lose you. I won't lie. Luka is still in my life, and you might not believe it, but he is nothing to me. I know—"

Jeannie could feel the tears starting to sting her eyes. She quickly ended the voicemail. Jeannie drew in a deep breath and pressed her lips together to stifle the tears she felt threatening to drop. Once she regained her composure, she continued walking down the road until she arrived at her house. Apologizing was out of the way. Now, she needed to figure out how to show Aaron with her actions that she could do better.

Once at home, she downed a cup of milk and got into bed. Her entire body ached, and painkillers weren't working anymore. There was no scientific explanation that Jeannie could think of to explain how Aaron's presence or embrace relieved her aching body, but they did. She missed him. Slowly, she drifted into a deep sleep.

When Jeannie opened her eyes, it was nighttime. Her phone was ringing, and she had left it on the kitchen counter. Reluctant at first, Jeannie dragged herself up from the bed and stretched. It didn't feel like it, but by looking at the clock, about five hours had passed. Jeannie craved a hot bath and then more sleep. She was sure that by the time she woke up the next morning, she'd be refreshed.

She reached her phone just in time to answer. It was a video call. When she saw Mason's name displayed on the screen, the sleep cleared from her eyes, and she answered quickly.

"Mason!"

One at a time, other faces popped up on the screen. It was a video call with Emily, Kelly, and Mason. From the look of things, they had been on the call long before she'd joined in. They immediately stopped talking when they heard her voice.

"Emily?" Jeannie said, taking a seat at the counter. She positioned her phone in the center of the table, holding it up with a glass cup.

"Hi, Mom," Emily said. "Did we wake you?"

Jeannie couldn't hold back the tears even though she tried. She covered her mouth with her hand and sobbed quietly.

"Oh, come on, mother," Emily continued. "Why are you crying now?"

"How could you be so cruel to me?" Jeannie sobbed. "Is this the way you treat your mother? You ignored me for weeks. You hurt me. I called you several times but no answer. If anyone should be angry with me, it shouldn't be you. You're supposed to understand me."

Emily paused. "I apologize, Mom. I admit that I was ignoring you, but only because I thought it would make you see reason."

"Stop crying already," Mason chimed on. "It's not like she was sick or anything. Plus, she was right to be angry with you because we told you, Mom. We were right."

Jeannie sniffed. "Told me what?"

"Mom, do you have your laptop with you?" Kelly asked. "We need you to open it and check your email."

"Where's Lily?" Jeannie asked.

"She didn't answer. We're guessing she thinks the video call is about her, so she's scared or something," Mason answered. "Mom, get your laptop."

"Alright. One second."

Jeannie wiped the tears from her eyes and went over to the

living room to grab her computer. She returned to the kitchen counter and turned it on.

"You said to check for what?" Jeannie asked.

"Your email," Emily answered. "Mason sent you an email twenty minutes ago. We've been waiting for you to answer the phone to talk about it."

Jeannie opened her mail and saw the message in question. She opened it and was immediately bombarded by several pictures, videos, and texts. Jeannie couldn't understand anything, and she had no idea where to start.

"What am I looking at?" Jeannie asked.

"Mason?" Emily called him quietly. "How about you explain?"

Jeannie heard Mason sigh through the phone. "Mom, calm down and listen to me. Don't get defensive, either," he started. "So, a week after Luka arrived in Chickadee Cove, Emily and I had a talk. Don't take this the wrong way, but Mom, you're terrible at reading people, and we were worried. We had seen Luka come and go from your life so many times and we didn't want that to happen again. We didn't want you falling into his trap again."

Jeannie was starting to understand where the conversation was going. The mail contained pictures of Luka partying, drinking, and playing in casinos with women. It was an intervention. For her.

"Guys," Jeannie said softly. "I am not getting back together with Luka. You don't have to do all of this. I know he womanizes and drinks and bets on games. I know. That's what you three don't want to understand. I don't love him anymore and nothing will change that."

"Mom," Emily said. "Those pictures are from two weeks ago, when Luka told you he was going to New York to see his doctor."

Jeannie's blood chilled. "What?"

"I hired a private investigator to follow Luka around a week after he arrived in Chickadee Cove. It was a collective decision by Emily, Kelly, and me. We gathered the money and paid him for weekly updates. He sent us all the information he had collected on Aaron three days ago, and we didn't know how to break it to you."

"He's not sick, Mom," Kelly added. "The hospital he claims to visit in New York has no record of him. I asked my husband for a favor, and he was the one who made investigations and told me. His pharmaceutical company supplies medications for that very hospital, so he knows the director personally. Luka had been there once before, to treat injuries he'd sustained when he had crashed a bike while drunk driving. That was years ago. He hasn't been there recently."

"He went to Las Vegas that week he told you he was meeting with his doctor. Those pictures are recent," Emily continued. "He spent all the time catching up with his friends, drinking with women, gambling, clubbing, and calling himself 'Sugar daddy Smith.' We're sorry, Mom. But this is just one of his tactics to get you back into his messy life."

Jeannie read the message exchange between Kelly's husband and the director of the hospital where he claimed that there was no record of Aaron's cancer prognosis anywhere. The only record they had of him dated back five years. If Jeannie recalled correctly, Luka wasn't even in her life at the time. She had no idea where he was. But apparently, he was in New York five years ago, and he approached her three years after.

"What is this?" she whispered. "What is going on?"

"We don't know what he wants with you," Mason explained. "But we are completely sure that he is telling you lies about his sickness. He's not sick, Mom. He never has been."

"I don't understand," Jeannie said with a quivering voice.

"Why? I need a reason. Why would he do all of this after our divorce? Why would he take his lie this far? Why?"

"That's what we have been trying to tell you, Mom," Emily explained. "Nothing makes sense when it comes to Luka. He is a dangerous, spontaneous person. I'm sure he just decided to test his skills. To see if he still has that control over you. He's bored."

"And he decided to play with me?"

"Is this enough reason to cut him off?" Emily asked. "Mom, I am serious when I say that if you don't—"

Jeannie covered her eyes, but it didn't stop the tears. She was boiling with anger but crushed by heartbreak. "Tell me the truth," she cried. "What do the three of you think of me? You think I'm unintelligent, don't you?"

"Oh, no, Mom," Kelly cooed. "We understand you, we just don't agree. Now that you know what Luka is up to, you can tell him off. That's all you needed. A reason. We've given it to you. This way, you won't feel guilty about anything."

"I ruined everything." Jeannie continued to cry. "You don't understand. I let him ruin my life again. This time, he didn't use my love for him or our children. He used death. Every single time, he comes up with ways to get to me and he succeeds. He always succeeds. I'm the foolish one here, and I hate how I am. I'm not even angry at Luka, I'm angry at myself. When I first moved to Chickadee Cove, I was convinced that Luka was behind me, but less than four months after I got here, I've managed to become who I was running from. I wanted to be independent, free, and at peace. Look at me now. I'm a walking mess."

"I won't let you blame yourself, Mom," Mason said. "Like you always say, you can't help how you are. Everything is Luka's fault. He's the vile man. Not you. It's not your fault. You might be easy to manipulate, Mom, but that's because you always put everyone else first. It's your first time trying to survive on your own. Away from us, newly divorced. You were bound to make mistakes. It's normal. Now you know. Take a stand. It might be hard to say no sometimes, but before you make a decision, put yourself first. That was the plan before you moved to Chickadee Cove, and you derailed from it."

The doorbell rang, startling Jeannie. She wiped her tears and stared at the door, already sure of who it was.

"Was that your door, Mom?" Kelly asked.

Jeannie nodded. "It's him. Luka. I wasn't at the shop today, and I'm sure he's here to pretend to worry about me."

"Do you need us to call Aunt Cathy? Or Aaron? I don't think you should talk to him alone," Mason said.

"Oh, I can talk to him alone," Jeannie said. "Stay on the call, guys. This should be quick."

Chapter Nineteen

"Y"ou will not be able to guess the surprise I have for you, Jeannie," were Luka's first words as soon as the door opened.

Jeannie felt alive all of a sudden. Knowing that it was finally over was a breath of fresh air. It was strange that she wasn't angry; rather, she was relieved at how much disgust she felt in that moment for Luka. The pity had dissipated, and the worry, too. This man wasn't chasing after her. He wanted her happiness. He wanted to ruin it.

Jeannie couldn't understand why Luka didn't want to see her happy. She had done nothing to him. Nothing at all. She cared for him, loved him at some point, and took care of their children. But all he did whenever he returned was take her happiness away. She should have known. She should have been the wiser.

"You know something, Luka?" Jeannie asked, standing at the door. "You...you are not human. I don't understand what you are, but you are not a real person."

Luka's smile waned. He stepped into the room and

crossed his arms. "What did Cathy have to say about me now?"

"Cathy?" Jeannie stepped into the room, too, and walked to him. "Cathy had a lot to say, I just didn't listen. I mean, what do you expect from a pushover like me? Someone so easy to manipulate. Someone you could toy with?"

"I don't know what lies Cathy or that construction guy must have told you, but I have no reason to lie to you, Jeannie. None at all."

"You still keep lying," Jeannie said. Deep down, she was enjoying the exchange, watching him lie when she knew the truth.

"Why would I lie to you?" Luka asked, slowly losing his patience.

"You tell me. That's what I want to know. Why have you been lying to me? To steal my happiness? To make me miserable? Why, Luka? I really need to know."

Luka took a step closer to her. "Have you been crying? Who made you cry? What did they say to you, Jeannie? What's got you so upset?"

Luka stroked her cheek with his fingers. His temerity amazed Jeannie, so much so that she couldn't close her mouth. How was this man so good at this? So good at deceit? Or perhaps, was it just her? Everyone else could see through his lies, but she never did. She always thought he could change. That he wanted to. But staring into his eyes in that moment confirmed everything. Jeannie had been such a fool.

"How, Luka?" she blurted. "Are you really a psychopath?"

Luka's eyebrows furrowed. "What?"

Jeannie smacked his hand away and stepped back. "You cried. You sobbed in my arms, trembling because you were scared you were going to die a miserable death. I believed you because how could I not?"

"What on God's green Earth are you talking about?" Luka asked. "Make me understand."

Jeannie crossed her arms. "You forget that your daughter is married to a big pharm guy, right?"

Luka raised his eyebrows and shook his head. "I'm lost."

"He knows hospitals. Directors. People with easy access to hospital records. Hill View Hospital? Kelly's husband knows the director. There's only one record of you. Five years ago. You've not been there since."

"I don't go to Hill View Hospital," Luka said.

"Oh, that's what you told me. Or have you forgotten? You said you were going for your tests there. You're going to lie about that, too?"

"I was going to go there, but I changed my mind," Luka stammered. "I went to Pearl Grace instead. It's in Soho, too. I can call my doctor and have him speak to you."

Jeannie snorted. It wasn't funny, and she was getting angry that he was holding on to his lie, but it amused her how far he was willing to go.

"Oh, Pearl Grace, you said?" Jeannie asked. "So, you don't mind if I call Kelly's husband to place a quick call through to someone there? I'm sure we'll confirm it in an hour whether you went there or not."

Luka scoffed. "Are you calling me a liar, Jeannie? Is that what this is? You're attacking me now? Is this how far you're willing to go to get rid of me? If you don't want me around you, just say it. I'm trying here. I am in pain every single day, but I am trying my best to make us work."

"Oh my God," Jeannie mumbled and began to pace the room. "Stop it. Just stop. Alright? I know already. Luka, I know you're not sick, and I know you're pretending. What I want to know is why you went through all of this hassle to ruin my life. Luka, I was fine on my own before you came. My life was near perfect. What did I ever do to you?"

"Call them," Luka said. "Make the call. Call Emily's husband."

"Kelly!" Jeannie yelled, losing her temper. "Kelly. You don't even—" she swallowed. "Get out."

"What?" Luka rasped.

"Luka, I want you to leave my house," Jeannie said. "I am not angry at you. I think you should be aware of that. What I feel right now is indifference. I couldn't care less what you do, why you did all that you did, what your motive was. I don't even want to know anymore. Just...leave."

"Jeannie, what is the matter with you? Talk to me. That's how you solve problems, by talking about them."

Jeannie sighed and slowly started to nod. "You were in Las Vegas, drinking with women, partying, gambling. I'm sure that's why you looked so sick when you got back. It wasn't the cancer, you were hung over."

"What?" Luka chuckled. "Oh my goodness. Where did you hear something so absurd?"

"There was a private investigator following you. He's been following you for weeks. We have pictures, videos, and evidence that you are not sick. Well...physically, you're not sick. Mentally, you are sick, Luka. The only issue is you haven't been diagnosed yet. But I am sure that if they checked, you have something."

Luka's smile began to wane. "You had someone follow me?" he rasped.

Jeannie smiled. "Why? You think I'm bluffing? Would you like to see the pictures? There're a ton of them. All dated. You were in Las Vegas when you said you were in New York. You never had cancer. You lied about that."

Luka clenched his jaw. He was speechless. For the first time since Jeannie had known him, Luka was speechless. She had backed him up to a corner finally. There was no denying it.

"I heard that I had three months to live," Luka started. "It broke me. So, I decided to have one last night of fun. Is that such a bad thing? To want to feel alive one last time before all the hair on my body falls out?"

Jeannie's eyebrows furrowed and her jaw practically dropped to the floor. She scoffed, and then scoffed again.

"Leave, Luka," Jeannie asked. "I will get a restraining order as soon as I can and if you so much as dare to step foot anywhere close to me, I will have you arrested. I don't deserve this. I'm not the most perfect person, and I am flawed, but I do not deserve this. I don't deserve you."

"Fine!" Luka roared. "So what? I don't have cancer. But what did you expect me to do? What was I supposed to do? Would you have listened to me? Would you have given me a chance if you didn't pity me?"

Jeannie's blood boiled at the same time as chills ran down her spine.

"You are a monster, Luka Smith."

"No, I am a man in love," he said, taking a step forward. "I am a man that loves you, Jeannie, and I will do anything to have you by my side. We have history. We have children. We are tied together forever, and no divorce paper will change that. You and me? It's for life. For better or for worse, remember? What? You can only stay when things are good, but when things get bad, you're allowed to move on with your life and abandon the world we built together? Is that what that construction guy told you?"

If Jeannie didn't know any better, she would have said that Luka was joking. He had to be. There was no way a real person had such a horrible mentality. He had so much to say now, and she had been rendered speechless, shut down by his audacity.

"Have you even asked yourself why I went to these lengths? Why I had to lie? To pretend to be what I am not?

Did you ask yourself why I was forced into doing all of this? It was all for you! For our family. Can you for once imagine what it would be like if our family was together again? Like we used to be? Stop thinking of yourself for once and start to think of other people."

"What?" Jeannie spat. "Are you insane? I put my life on hold because of you! I sacrificed my happiness for almost thirty years because of you. Luka, you came back into my life and caused this much havoc, all for what?"

"Please, don't pretend you didn't do it for yourself," Luka retorted. "You did it for your conscience. Because you didn't want to feel guilty in case I died alone after begging you to be with me in my last moments. You didn't take any of the blame. You were being selfish."

"Get out!" Jeannie screamed. "Leave. Right now."

Luka mellowed and took a few steps back. "Calm down. Think of Lily. Think of our daughter. She is young, fragile. I already told her that we were patching things up between us. That's all she has ever wanted. That's her dream. Think of how our fighting will affect her. If you have to pretend, then do so. But you know how Lily is."

"Luka," Jeannie said, glaring at him. "Get out of my life. I refuse to be driven to insanity because of you. I'm being selfish with my happiness. I don't care what you told Lily. Handle it yourself. Go away. Just know that you have ruined any possible chance of receiving help from me in any way. If you were drowning and I had a rope, I would watch you go under."

"You don't mean that," Luka responded.

"You'd believe that," Jeannie said and scoffed. "But I'm trying something new. Something where I show people what I mean in actions rather than in words. So, I'd advise that for your own good, don't need me for anything. I will not help. Whatever you want to do about Lily, do it. When you break her heart, I'll be here to comfort her. I am her mother after all. She'll always come back to me."

"You don't care if she tries to kill herself?"

"You made her like this!" Jeannie yelled. "It's all your fault and you keep forgetting it. Leave, Luka. Or else I'll scream and attract the neighbors."

"I can't leave just yet," he answered.

"Luka, get out."

"I can't," he said again. "I can't leave just yet."

"And why not? You want me to push you out?"

Luka sighed. "You haven't asked what my surprise is."

Jeannie squinted her eyes. "Surprise? Do I look like I am in the mood for surprises? You are a joke, Luka. I am this close to calling the police."

"Just..." Luka swallowed. "You really need to calm down. If you don't, then this won't go well."

Luka walked over to the corner of the room and made a phone call. He was too relaxed for her liking. Like he had a backup plan, almost as if this was just some stumbling block he could overcome. Jeannie wondered what she had done to give him such confidence that he was there to stay in her life.

"Mom! Oh my God."

Jeannie was stunned to silence when Lily ran into the room and embraced her. She froze, unable to wrap her head around the fact that Lily was there in the same room with her.

"Oh, you don't know how excited I am, Mom," Lily beamed, jumping up and down. "When Dad told me you both had reconciled, I didn't believe it. But it's true, and it's freaking me out. I'm so glad you are giving him another chance, Mom. You both are going to be so happy, and you'll grow old together. I just know it."

Jeannie was unsure what Luka had told Lily. From her excitement and her jolly tone, it didn't seem as though she knew. Evidently, the only lie he told Lily was that they had reconciled.

"Your Mom and I are taking things slow," Luka chimed in. He placed his hand on Lily's back and rubbed it. "That's why we're not living together at the moment. We're starting from the beginning. But I know that soon, all of that will change."

"Lily, where did you come from?" Jeannie asked.

"My plane landed an hour ago, and Dad picked me up from the airport. It was supposed to be our surprise. He said you missed me and you were whining to him about how much you wanted to see me. So, here I am! I cleared my schedule and I came here for you, mummy. Aren't you excited?"

"To see you? Absolutely," Jeannie said. "But your father was just leaving. You're staying here with me, right? Where are your bags?"

"They are at Dad's place," Lily answered. "It doesn't matter where I stay. We're together. As a family again."

It was time to end Lily's misconceptions about the relationship. It was time for her to finally grow up. Luka's antics at sowing seeds of lies in Lily's heart completely disgusted her.

"Lily, your father has been lying to you," Jeannie started.

"Jeannie, don't," Luka rasped, taking a step forward and placing himself between them.

Jeannie shoved him aside and placed both hands on Lily's shoulders. "I dislike your father. I detest him. You know all those times you used to ask me why you were like this? Or what was wrong with you? Well, it's all your father's fault."

"Jeannie," Luka rasped again.

"Your father is an unrepentant liar and unsalvageable cheat," Jeannie told Lily. "And he ruined all our lives."

Chapter Twenty

"Don't listen to her, Lily," Luka said, shoving Jeannie away. "She is jealous of our relationship. She's trying to keep me away from you. We talked about this."

"Listen to Mom, you idiot!"

The sound of Kelly's voice echoed across the room. Jeannie had forgotten that her children were still on the call, listening to everything.

"What was that?" Lily asked, scurrying to the kitchen. She picked up the phone and brought it to her face. "Mason? Emily? Kelly? What's going on?"

"For once, Lily, listen," Emily said. "You never do, and you take after Mom in that regard. Stand your ground and listen to the truth. Have you not wondered why we are so hell bent on you staying away from Luka? Do you think it's only because he was an absentee dad?"

"It's majorly because of what he did to you," Kelly added. "You are the primary reason we don't like him. Listen."

"Me?"

Visibly confused, Lily set the phone down and turned to

the two adults in the room. She stared back and forth at them in silence waiting to hear what they had to say about what her siblings had just said.

"Well?" she finally said. "I am so confused right now."

Luka exhaled loudly and took a step forward. "Lily, my darling—"

"Not you, Dad," Lily said, raising a hand in the air. "Thinking about it, I've only listened to what you have to say for the past year. I've done all you asked of me. I think I want to hear what Mom has to say."

Jeannie shut her eyes tightly to fight back the stinging tears. She walked over to Lily, sat her down on the kitchen counter, and stood in front of her.

"It was 16 years ago," Jeannie started. "Back in New York. You were only two years old. Luka had returned to our lives for the umpteenth time and as usual, I had been deceived into thinking he was there to stay. He came with the lies prepared, the self-pity, the guilt-filled eyes. You liked your father even at that age because he had his way with you. He still has a way with you apparently, since you still like him now."

Lily sat up and straightened her back.

"Luka had this shtick, and he still has it. It's one where he'd try his hardest during the first month or two to convince me that he was going to stay for good. He'd be the perfect husband, run errands, do all sorts of things until I got comfortable. This time, he was serious with you, since Mason, Emily, and Kelly didn't want to be around him. He was putting on this act to be the perfect dad for you. So, I let him. One fateful day, we had scheduled for Luka to pick you up from daycare. I usually did it, but he insisted that he was going to. He didn't."

Lily raised one eyebrow. "What? He didn't pick me up from daycare? That's it?"

"Listen!" Emily and Mason chorused.

"He went drinking instead and forgot," Jeannie continued. "I called him constantly, countless times, but I got no answer. When he finally answered the phone, he claimed that he had picked you up. That you were with him at the park. So, I let it go and went back to work. A few hours later, he called me. Luka asked me if I had picked you up from school. That's when I knew he had messed up. That we were in trouble. You were gone, Lily. Your bags were still at the daycare, and your shoes. But you were gone."

"What?" Lily breathed. "What do you mean...gone?"

"You had been kidnapped," Mason chimed in. "There was a community-wide search for you."

"Mom collapsed so many times, we couldn't keep count. She lost so much weight during that period," Emily said. "I'm sure we can still find the story on the internet if we search for it."

"What? Where was I? Why don't I remember this?"

"The doctor said it happens when a child gets traumatized," Jeannie explained. "You didn't talk for months, Lily."

"How did..." Lily stammered. "How was I..."

"It took three days before the police found you," Jeannie explained. "In a trash can. Apparently, the people who took you abandoned you there. No explanation whatsoever. You had some bruises on your arm, a burn, but other than that, you were fine physically. The police couldn't explain why they abandoned you. Lily, you had to be hospitalized for weeks. You see that burn on your thigh? That scar?"

"It was from that?" Lily asked with a quivering voice.

"It was."

"Where was Dad in all of this?" Lily asked, turning to stare at him.

Jeannie glared at him, then turned back to Lily. "After the call, when I told him that I didn't pick you up from school, and he confirmed that you were missing, he disappeared again. He made no effort to look for you."

"He just vanished, like he always does," Mason said. "A sad excuse for a man, if you ask me."

"But you forgot all about the incident," Jeannie said. "When you turned four, you started asking for your dad and throwing tantrums. We couldn't possibly tell you what happened at that age, so we just let you miss him. Then he came back fifteen years later, armed with the excuse that he had been so traumatized by what he did that he couldn't bring himself to come back home. That was when I divorced him and we parted ways. I had seen through all of his bullshit then, but little did I know that two years later, he'd still have a trick up his sleeve. This might be harsh of me to say to you, but all Luka ever did was abandon us. He doesn't deserve to be close to my children, and he surely doesn't deserve any compassion from me or you. Lily, you were a cheerful child when you were two years old. You were the brightest. A ray of sunshine. But after that incident, you didn't talk for months, you stopped smiling, and things just went downhill from there. Till this day, we don't know what happened to you."

Lily rose to her feet and confronted Luka. "Aren't you going to say something?" she asked. "Or are you just going to stand there in silence?"

"Lily," he said quietly. He had water in his eyes, and if she didn't know who he really was, Jeannie would have been fooled. "I know all of this sounds terrible, but I promise you, I never intended to hurt you. It was a mistake."

"Was abandoning me also a mistake?" Lily asked. "They say you didn't even search for me."

"Do you know how hurt I was?" Luka asked. "I could barely sleep for months. It tormented me, and that's why I stayed away for so long. I was ashamed."

"So, it's true?" Lily asked. She had started to hyperventilate. "It's true?"

"I'm here now," Luka said. "I promise I won't abandon you now."

Lily swung her handbag at him and screamed at the top of her lungs. Her entire body was trembling, and she was red all over. She stormed out of the house as fast as she could and slammed the door behind her.

"Lily!" Jeannie yelled.

They both ran after her, but they weren't fast enough. Lily had already gotten into Luka's car and locked the doors.

"She's got the key," Luka announced.

"What?"

"What was I supposed to do? Leave her in the car and take the keys?" Luka asked.

Before Jeannie could react, Lily zoomed off at high speed. The car swerved left and right until she took a hard turn at the corner and disappeared.

"Lily!" Jeannie screamed, panicking.

Lily wasn't stable. The last thing she ought to be doing was driving.

"What are we going to do?" Luka asked. "She shouldn't be driving, Jeannie. Something terrible could happen. Lily is a very erratic person."

"Shut up!" Jeannie lashed at him. "We are not going to do anything. I am. Leave us alone, Luka. It's what you do best. This time, I'm asking you. Go away."

Jeannie couldn't control her shaking. She was already imagining a car crash with Lily in it. Lily herself was even capable of driving the car over a cliff. It wasn't the first time she had tried to kill herself, and now they had just given her a good reason to try again.

"Mason, Emily, Kelly, I have to go," Jeannie announced,

picking up the phone with shaking hands. "Lily just drove off and I have no idea where she's going and she's not stable."

Without giving her children time to react, Jeannie ended the call and instinctively dialed Aaron's number. He was the only person she thought to call, and she didn't even take into consideration the fact that he was actively ignoring her.

"Jeannie."

A sigh of relief coursed through her body. "Aaron, thank God you answered. I—"

"I'm here."

The voice was clearer now, and it took Jeannie a few seconds before she realized that Aaron was standing in the same room with her. He stood at the door with his phone to his ear. From the way he looked, it was obvious that he had left home in a hurry. He had on slippers, black shorts, and a hoodie.

Jeannie stared at him with tears streaming down her cheeks. There were so many emotions she was feeling at that moment, but the one that overshadowed the others was relief. After over a week, Aaron had finally called her name again.

"Mason called me a while ago," Aaron explained. "He said you were going to confront Luka and he didn't want you to do it alone. So I came here to help, but...why are you crying? Did he do something? If he did, then you better say it now, because I just saw him leaving and I bet I can catch up with him."

Jeannie ran to him and wrapped her arms around his waist. She sobbed uncontrollably like a child throwing a tantrum.

"Lily's in trouble," she managed to say. "It's Lily."

Aaron pulled away from the embrace and held her at arm's length. "Lily? What happened to Lily?"

"Luka tried to use her to emotionally blackmail me into a relationship with him, but I, in turn, told Lily a secret I had kept from her for years. It broke her heart and she drove off. She's unstable, Aaron. She shouldn't be driving, and I'm worried, I don't have a car to go in search for her. I don't know what to do."

"Alright calm down," Aaron told her. "Lily might be unstable, but you can't be. You need a level head to look for her. I brought my car, we'll start the search for her. I'll call some of my friends at the police station to alert dispatch to keep an eye out for Luka's car. You call Cathy and anyone else with a car that can help.

"I'll call Sarah, she's the baker at the bakery. She has a car."

"Good. What does Luka's car look like?" Aaron asked.

Jeannie shook her head as she tried to think. "It's a black Ford. The plate number had AAA in it, two fives...I can't recall the rest of it."

"Where's Luka going?" Aaron asked. "Shouldn't this be the part where he stays and helps?"

"I asked him to leave," Jeannie said. "I'd rather die than ask him for help. Lily's my child and my child alone. I'll find her myself."

"Good," Aaron said. "Let's go."

Together, they started the search for Lily while Jeannie made some calls. It was late, but Cathy responded and left the house with her husband to search the area for any signs of Lily. Sarah didn't hesitate to leave the house. She told Jeannie she was going to pick up Denice, and they'd both search their area, too.

"You know, this reminds me of that incident sixteen years ago," Jeannie sobbed. "This was how it started. I called neighbors, the police...we all started searching for Lily all through the night. It's like I'm reliving it."

"Lily has gone missing before?" Aaron asked.

"She has been kidnapped before," Jeannie said. "I was

going to tell you about it, but it never really came up. Probably because I try so hard to forget it."

"We'll find her," Aaron assured Jeannie. "Don't worry."

Jeannie turned to him. "Aaron, I'm so sorry, I—"

"No." Aaron shook his head. "We're not talking about us tonight. We can talk when we find Lily. That's the priority. Don't worry about how I'm feeling. You can tell me everything I need to know later."

Jeannie nodded in response and cried quietly. After hours of searching, Lily and Aaron decided to search the woods. Jeannie couldn't tell how long she'd walked for, but she only stopped when her phone buzzed in her pocket.

"Jeannie, we couldn't find the car, or her," Cathy said. "We've searched all night. I don't think she came this way. It's almost five in the morning, and the kids will soon be awake. Once they are ready for school and I send them off, we will continue the search. Don't worry too much, alright?"

It was only when Cathy pointed it out that Jeannie realized how much time had passed.

"Thank you," she answered weakly. "Thank you so much."

There was no sign of Lily hours after she had driven off. Jeannie stood in the middle of the woods quivering. If anything were to happen to Lily, it was going to be all her fault. Jeannie looked around for Aaron and then realized he wasn't with her. She needed to find him quickly. She wasn't feeling so good. She couldn't keep her head still. She tried leaning on a tree, but as her head touched the trunk, darkness started to pervade. Her legs gave way. The last thing she felt was her body hitting the ground.

"Jeannie, are you awake? Can you hear me?"

The light was blinding, but Jeannie managed to open her eyes. She sprung up from the couch and frantically scanned the room.

"Lily? Aaron, where's Lily?" she breathed. "What time is it? Did you find her? What happened?"

Aaron caressed her arm. "Calm down, alright? We couldn't find Lily, but I have people searching for her. We can't make an official case with the police until after forty-eight hours, but I have friends in the force searching for her, too. It's currently 9 a.m. You passed out in the woods."

Jeannie placed her hand on her head. "I'm scared, Aaron. I am terrified."

Aaron was about to respond when his phone rang and interrupted them. "It's my friend in the police force," Aaron said. "I'll put it on speaker."

"Mr. Horn. We found the car," the man announced over the phone. "Registered to one Luka Smith, and it matches the description you gave us."

Jeannie grabbed the phone and staggered to her feet. "Hello, sir, this is the mother of the passenger in the vehicle. Is she alright? Please, where is she?"

"The car is wrecked, ma'am. We found it on the side of the highway."

Jeannie's blood chilled. With her heart in her mouth, Jeannie asked in almost a whisper, "And the passenger? The young lady?"

"There was no one in the car when we arrived, ma'am," the officer answered. "There's blood and a bag where we found a lady's phone, but we cannot find the driver."

Jeannie's knees gave way and she crashed to the floor.

"Where's Lily?" she asked him with a quivering voice.

About the Author

Eliza's a BIG believer in love. She writes sweet romances that make you swoon, laugh and believe in love again.

A mother of two children, Eliza and her husband of twenty-five years live in NH. She enjoys spending time with them and taking care of her many pets. When she isn't working on her next book, you can find her at the local nursery looking for the next hybrid tea rose to add to her garden.

www.ingramcontent.com/pod-product-compliance
Lightning Source LLC
Chambersburg PA
CBHW071322140726
47996CB00005B/1778